1754

ILLEGAL ENTRY

By Robert Bernard

Robert Bernard

ILLEGAL
ENTRY

W·W·NORTON&COMPANY·INC·

New York

F I R S T   E D I T I O N

Copyright © 1972 by Robert Bernard Martin. All rights reserved. Published simultaneously in Canada by George J. McLeod Limited, Toronto. Printed in the United States of America.

Library of Congress Catalog Card No. 75-169041

SBN 393 08662 3

1 2 3 4 5 6 7 8 9 0

For G'Ann

ILLEGAL ENTRY

CHAPTER ONE

ALTHOUGH HE HAD SPLASHED THEM with cold water, his eyes still felt puffy as he stumbled back down the aisle. Air travel was the invention of the devil. Particularly transatlantic flights at night. Takeoff at Kennedy at eleven in the evening, then cocktails at twelve-fifteen. Cocktails at a quarter past midnight! A bad dinner half an hour later, an hour or two of sleep before the stewardess woke him to push a plate of plastic breakfast under his nose. And now they were over the Bristol Channel, already beginning the descent toward London. He felt like hell, but he knew that when he saw Jim waiting at the exit from the Customs hall he would forget his fatigue.

As he sat down, the sign flashed on. Seat belts. He put out a cigarette. The NO SMOKING light had not yet come on, but his mouth tasted terrible. "Yes, it's been a good flight," he lied, in answer to the man beside him, with whom he had talked during intervals of wakefulness. "My name is Stevenson," his seatmate had introduced himself. He was a Liverpool manufacturer, returning from a visit to a married daughter in New York.

By stretching, he could see out of the window, past Mr. Stevenson, and watch the wing of the plane assume a sickening angle as they approached London. Beneath him spread the delicate gray-green of southern England, compounded of pale crops in the little fields, the darker shades of the hedgerows, and the smoky haze that softened colors without obscuring them. The gray roofs of the western part of the country had given place to the reddish tiles of Buckinghamshire. Even from an airplane, it would be impossible to mistake this countryside for any other in the world.

Land and people merged in this ancient little country to

form something distinctly English. Mike knew that he would recognize the nationality of the man beside him without hearing him speak, even if he were dressed like an Arab or a Greek. The reddish cheeks, clear blue eyes, wide and sympathetic mouth, even the wart covered with long pale hairs by his left ear: all were as immediately and verifiably English as a passport. Probably his ancestors were Danish, French, Celtic, perhaps Roman, but centuries ago the blood of intermingled nations had coalesced into something more distinct than any of its components.

In another hundred years Jim's descendants would be impossible to distinguish from other Englishmen whose ancestors had been here since the Conquest. He hoped that Angela would be with Jim at the gate. He wanted to get to know his brother's fiancée as soon as possible. That would be a pleasure if she were as charming as Jim claimed. Worth waiting for until he was twenty-eight, Jim had written. He hoped that the shambles of his own marriage wouldn't depress them. Not that many engaged couples ever seemed to worry about the failures of others in matrimony; they always knew that their own marriage would be different. And Jim's and Angela's probably would be, too. Already Jim seemed to have steadied down a lot. He'd lost the radical ideas that used to be so annoying, and he seemed much more secure and happy. At least until this last letter.

He pulled it out of an inner pocket and reread it for the hundredth time. Most of it was about Angela and their plans to get married later in the year; the last paragraphs had prompted this flight:

> There's something damned funny going on around here, Mike, and I'm pretty upset about it. What I've been working on is secret, of course, but I can tell you that it would revolutionize the airplane industry if it's as good as I think. The trouble is that it would make a lot of changes in the petroleum industry, too. It would be fine for Coronado, but it would raise hell with some of the other companies. What's got me upset is that someone has been going through my records. There are five of us

on this operation, but I'm in charge of coordinating the work, and I work immediately under the Director, reporting to him. It's been kept very secret, and even the other four men working with me don't know the scope of the whole thing.

As soon as I was positive that someone had been at the records I went to the Director, who has been great to me ever since I got here. Maybe I'm too nervous, but I think he's too easygoing. He acted as if I were imagining the whole thing and suggested that I needed a rest after I finished writing up the work, which I should do by next week. I don't mind a rest, but I'll be damned if I'm imagining anything. Even Angela thinks I've been working too hard and that there's probably nothing in the whole thing. I wish to hell you were here to talk to. It's got nothing to do with nationality, but for the first time since I've been here, I really feel like an alien, as if no one understood me. You would.

It had taken Mike only twenty-four hours to decide to have his vacation in England earlier than he had planned. The next morning he had made his reservations and sent a cable to Jim, asking him to meet the plane if possible.

As he folded the letter and put it back in his pocket, he saw Mr. Stevenson looking with concern at him. "Nothing the matter, is there, lad? You look worried. I hope England is going to be a pleasure for you." The faint lilt of the Northern Country accent lent additional concern to the kindness of the question.

"It will be." Mike smiled, successfully he hoped. "England's always a pleasure."

"Let me know if there's anything I can do. We Englishmen like our guests to be happy."

There was something so spontaneously sympathetic about the words that Mike found himself talking more than was his habit with strangers. "There's nothing you can do, thanks, but as a matter of fact, I'm a little worried about this trip." He patted his coat pocket, where he had put the letter. "I have a brother

living in England, and I'm going to visit him. He seems to be
having a little trouble." He smiled again. "But I'm sure it's nothing serious."

The loudspeaker prevented further conversation. "Please
remain in your seats until the aircraft has come to a complete
halt and the engines have stopped." English stewardesses always
sounded as if they were hoping for a break on the stage. This
one wasn't even English; she was a nice Welsh girl, whose native
woodnotes came through the affected Southern English as
startlingly as the dark roots of her hair contrasted with the
blond curls that surmounted them. Why couldn't they leave
nature unadorned? Even the Liverpool accent of the man beside
him was pleasanter than her hybrid speech.

With an almighty bang the landing gear snapped out of the
plane's intestines and fixed into place. "It is now ten-twenty-
three London time, and the airport temperature is fifty-seven
degrees. The duty-free liquor will be available as you go through
Customs. We hope you have had a pleasant journey. Thank you."
He felt in his pocket for the receipt for the bourbon he had
bought at Kennedy. In spite of three years in England and an
English fiancée, his brother hadn't lost his taste for the best of
Kentucky. Good to know, too, that it wouldn't be as hot as it had
been in New York. It would make it easier to get through the
day after an almost sleepless night.

He crossed his fingers in an involuntary childish gesture as
the plane dipped its nose and headed straight for the runway
and the distant buildings of the airport. Takeoffs were the real
danger, he knew, but landings frightened him more. In spite of
himself he caught his breath and held it until the wheels made
surprisingly gentle contact with the ground. He relaxed as the
plane seemed to lose its sense of direction and head away from
the main group of buildings. At the end of the field it wheeled
back, its engines now settled to a tolerable roar, and taxied
toward a side strip.

In flagrant disregard of the stewardess's warning, Mike's
seatmate was already on his feet, his belt disengaged. "Sorry,"
he said as he stepped on Mike's feet and struggled toward the
aisle. Amused, Mike sat quietly and watched him take down his

coat and two or three hand parcels. There was no need to hurry. They still had to get onto the little airport bus to go to the terminal. After the plane came to a stop, he remained sitting until almost all the other passengers had gone down the aisle. At last he stood up and got his hat, coat, and one small bag, and walked comfortably toward the door. He was the last down the ramp and stepped into the waiting bus. All the seats were taken, but his leisurely exit from the plane meant that he would be the first out of the bus on its arrival at the terminal.

Ahead of the others he walked briskly down the winding corridors of the terminal. With any luck he should be looking for the beaming face of his younger brother in another ten minutes. He had only one bag, enough to keep him decent for a short visit, and he had nothing to declare, so that he could walk directly through the Customs gate unless he was picked out for inspection. Arrival in England was a hell of a lot pleasanter than it was in one of the big American international airports. Even the Immigration and Customs officials were obliging. Maybe the difference between ninety-five degrees in New York and fifty-seven in London accounted for the contrast between one's welcome in the two places.

A pretty girl in uniform stood at the first gate he approached, that of the health authorities, but she merely handed him a card and said, "I hope you will have a pleasant visit in England." She didn't have to ask whether he was English; his clothes told her that he was not. She waved him toward the queue for non-British passports. There were four Immigration officers sitting at otherwise empty desks, and the one nearest him beckoned. This was even easier and quicker than he had dared to hope.

"May I have your landing card and passport, please?" The young man behind the desk gave him a friendly, impersonal smile. Mike handed him the documents, and the officer asked, without looking at them, "How long will you be in England?"

"Three weeks."

"And what's the purpose of your trip?"

"I'm visiting my brother." He hoped he had picked the best bourbon; he was a Scotch drinker himself.

Smiling, the officer looked at the passport photo, then up at Mike. "Not very flattering, is it, Mr. Templeman?"

"I got it in a hurry. It's not much worse than my passport pictures usually are." He grinned in return, envying the English their public officials.

The man was studying Mike's passport, and his smile slowly faded. He reached for a thick black book and flipped to a page near the back, looked at it, then glanced again at the passport. A frown came over his face. "Wait here, please."

"Sure. What's the matter?"

The official turned and made a slight signal with his hand to the policeman standing at the door of the Customs room. "I want to check with one of my superiors. Wait here, please." He scooped up the passport and landing card and went out of a nearby door.

Mike shifted his weight to his left foot. Surely there was nothing wrong with the passport, even if he had got it in a hurry. The Passport Division in Washington was far more efficient than it had once been, and he hadn't heard of its making mistakes. Not unintentional ones, at least. He craned his neck to look upside down at the black book, but there was nothing on its cover to indicate its contents. As he looked up, he saw the unwinking stare of the policeman at the door, fixed on him.

By now almost all the passengers had arrived from the plane, and the other desks were busy. He turned around and saw Mr. Stevenson at the head of a nearby queue for British subjects. Stevenson waved with a friendly smile, but some of the people in the queue behind Mike were stirring impatiently and glaring. With unusual petulance, he glared back. It wasn't his fault. He wished the Immigration officer would come back. Jim was a busy man, and he hated to keep him waiting.

The door through which the young official had disappeared opened, and he returned, followed by a policeman and an older man in uniform. As they approached, Mike asked, "What's the trouble?"

"Are you Mr. Templeman?" Mike nodded to the older man. "Would you come with me please?" Already the first official was beckoning to the next man in line, who hurried forward in impatient relief.

"Come along, please." His tone was markedly less friendly than that of the first man.

Mike silently followed him out the door, accompanied by the policeman, then down a corridor. "In here, please." The official waved him into a small office to which the door stood open. Mike went in and sat in the chair that the officer indicated. The policeman stood by the door as the other man went around the desk and sat down.

"Mr. Michael Yelton Templeman."

"Yes, I told you that."

"Born in Connecticut?" He pronounced it "Connekticut."

"Yes. It says so right there." Mike pointed at the passport. Better if he could keep the annoyance out of his voice.

"Where in Connekticut?"

"Greenwich."

"This is a new passport, isn't it?"

"Yes."

"And a new passport picture?"

"Yes, I had it taken when I applied for the passport a month or so ago."

"But you had a mustache then. And you haven't got one now."

Mike's first reaction was to remain silent, but the other man's voice clearly implied a question. "Yes, I got tired of it. I had had it only six months or so, and I thought I'd cut it off before I came to see my brother."

"Is your brother English?"

For a moment Mike had to hold onto himself. Then he relaxed. Officials were the same everywhere. Only a few minutes ago he had been complaining to himself about American officialdom. "No, he's American, but he's lived here for three years."

"What's his name? Where does he live?"

"James Templeman. He lives in Market Doddington. In Warwickshire."

"What's his occupation?"

"He's a research chemist. He works for Coronado Petroleum."

During the questioning the other man had not looked up at Mike, and his expression did not change at the answers. "What's your occupation?"

"Lawyer."

"Why did you come to visit your brother?"

Mike's temper had been held in check too long. "For Christ's sake, why does a brother come to visit a brother? Because he's my brother. And because he recently got engaged, and I wanted to meet his fiancée. Not that I think that's any of your business."

"Don't get excited, Mr. Templeman. It is our business. I'm sorry, but I'm afraid I can't give you permission to stay in England."

"Why not?" Mike was almost shouting now.

"We don't have to tell you that. Visiting Great Britain is a privilege, and we don't have to explain if we withdraw that privilege."

For a second or two Mike was mute with fury before he burst out: "Then, for God's sake, let me get in touch with the American Embassy. They will see that I get to stay."

"I could let you phone them, but I can promise that there is nothing they could do. Would you prefer to return to the United States or to continue your flight to some other country?"

"God damn it, neither one. I want to stay here. My brother is waiting for me, and I intend to see him."

"I'm afraid that's impossible." The Immigration officer looked at him blandly, quite unperturbed by the flash of temper. "But, as I say, you have got the choice of returning to America or continuing your trip. Which would you prefer? If you like, you can take some time to make up your mind and let me know later. This officer will take you to another room, and you can make yourself comfortable there while you decide." He stood up and nodded to the policeman, who had not yet spoken.

"Aren't you even willing to discuss this with me?"

"There's nothing further to say, Mr. Templeman. Any discussion would waste both our times. I'm only following orders. Besides, I'm afraid I'm rather busy today. And now, if you don't mind . . ." He pointed to the door.

Mike walked over to the desk and reached for his passport, but before he could take it, the other had picked it up. "This will be given back to you when you leave. And please leave your suitcase here."

"You'll hear more about this kind of treatment," Mike threatened as he started toward the door.

"Quite possibly" was all the answer he got, as the man began reading one of the papers on his desk.

Mike followed the policeman to a stark little office containing a bench and two chairs. He took one of the chairs and threw his raincoat down on the bench. "What's all this about?" he demanded of the policeman.

"Couldn't say, sir," answered the guardian of Her Majesty's law, and stared out of the window at a great flight of steps slowly being trundled past by a tractor.

Once he had left the official, Mike began to regain control of his temper. He had no idea why he had been picked out of the line, but there was evidently nothing that he could do about it now. On the whole, it would be better to go on to the Continent. Perhaps Jim could come over there to join him. Anyway, he had come all this way for part of his vacation, and it would be pointless to get on a plane for New York. "All right, then, I'll go to Paris."

Without answering, the policeman picked up a telephone and gave Mike's message. Within a minute or two the senior official came back into the office. "I think this is a sensible decision, Mr. Templeman," he said. "If you don't mind trusting me with your money, I'll arrange your flight." Wordlessly, Mike pulled out a traveler's check and signed it before handing it over.

"Can you at least do me the favor of taking a message to my brother? Will you tell him that I'm not permitted to land, and that I'm going on to Paris? I'll call him from there."

"Where had you arranged to meet him?"

"At the exit from Customs. He'll be with a young lady, I think."

"Very well. If he is there, I'll see that he gets the message." The official paused before leaving the room, as if there were something he wanted to tell Mike. Then he appeared to think better of his impulse. "But I doubt that he'll be there." He left without waiting for a reply.

In another hour Mike had been given back his passport, his case, and the change left from the purchase of the ticket. In a last attempt to get an explanation, he said as his passport was handed to him, "I don't understand why you're treating me like this. I haven't done anything."

For a moment the official face lost its impersonality. "No. No, I don't suppose you have." The officer turned away, and Mike went through the barrier to the Paris-bound plane.

Tired as he was, it still seemed foolish to attempt to sleep on such a short flight. When he got to Paris, he would call Jim, have a good French dinner, and sleep for twelve hours. He reached under his seat and slid out his flat suitcase. Before leaving home he had bought a paperback copy of *Vanity Fair*, which he had not read in years, to comfort him during the flight, but he had been too tired to take it out over the Atlantic. As he opened the case now, he saw the inappropriate cover of the book, decorated with a young woman whose bust swelled out of an anachronistic eighteenth-century bodice. Hardly the Amelia he remembered. Or was it meant to be Becky? His amusement came to a sudden stop as he remembered that he had placed the book in the section that held his extra suit. Now it was resting on the shirts in the other section. He knew that he had not opened the suitcase during the flight. The Immigration officials must have searched it. Damn officialdom. He should have locked the case before getting on the plane.

He poked through its scanty contents. Nothing else appeared to have been disturbed. As he picked up the book, it fell open in his hands, its spine cracked. He felt nearly as annoyed at the clumsy handling of the book as he did at the search of his suitcase. It was always annoying to read a paperback with a broken spine.

Perhaps it was childish to be so put off by a ham-handed official's awkwardness, but the thought that the book had recently been searched dampened his enthusiasm for Thackeray at the moment. A stewardess passed, handing out London newspapers. There would be time for the novel later.

As he unfolded the afternoon paper, a headline caught his eye: "AMERICAN DESERTS TO RUSSIANS?" The story was short but sufficient:

Officials at the Market Doddington Research Centre of Coronado Petroleum, Ltd., today indicated that James Templeman, 28, American chemist who was employed in top-secret research on a project jointly sponsored by Coronado and the Government, had been missing for several days. Templeman had been working for almost three years on the project with English chemists.

No comment was yet available from either the Home Office or the Foreign Office, but it was reliably understood that several Members intended to ask the Government in the House why Templeman, who is said to have been a Communist while he was an undergraduate, was given clearance to come to this country to work on a top-secret research project. Mr. Gerald Packington, M.P. for Ounster, said today that this was only the latest in a series of outrages perpetrated on British security by careless information from the United States.

The Director of the Market Doddington Centre was unavailable for comment, but a member of his staff said that Templeman's pro-Russian sympathies were well known, and that since his disappearance there was speculation as to whether he had deserted to Russia. Several important papers were said to be missing since Templeman had vanished.

Mrs. Mary Stubbins, Templeman's landlady, said that she first discovered his absence two days ago. She assumed that he had gone off on a trip connected with his work, until she was asked by a member of the Research Centre whether he was ill. She said that his rent had been paid in advance.

So far there has been no official announcement about Templeman. The U.S.S.R. embassy refused to comment, saying that it had no knowledge of Templeman, either now or in the past.

CHAPTER TWO

OH, MY GOD!" Mike said involuntarily at the pain. He doubled
over and rubbed ineffectually at his knee. It would probably
be swollen and sore, and he needed to be at his physical best.

"I'm most dreadfully sorry, I really am. I *do* hope you're
all right." The old woman stopped in her flight and swung
around to face him. Mike hastily moved his leg, to keep from
having it hit again by the string bag of bottles that dangled from
her left hand. She paused irresolutely, looked wildly back at
the ship, which was hooting in preparation for casting off. "I
can't stop. I must catch the boat. I'm *so* sorry!" She turned and
headed toward the Channel steamer, her chubby legs moving in
a half trot, her ridiculously tiny red hat threatening to part
company with her iron-gray hair, her indubitably English tweed-
clad arms flapping as they attempted to hang on to the parcels
she carried. He hoped she wouldn't have a heart attack. "So
sorry" floated back to him on the wind. "Wait, wait! Attendez,
attendez!" The latter was presumably directed to the dock
workers to whom she was waving her packages desperately.

Mike stood rubbing at his knee and watched her chaotic
flight. She was not a sight to ignore, and even the dockers,
hardened as they must be by now, stared in fascination. The
steamer was just beginning to slide away from the dock, but the
gangplank had not yet been drawn up, and with one final leap
she cleared the distance between it and the dock, landing on her
knees, then slowly toppling forward, her nose among the
parcels, exposing an unseemly amount of sensible underwear.
Then, improbably, she rose to her feet and walked in disorderly
dignity to the deck of the ship. For a moment she disappeared
from sight behind the rail before she stood erect, her arms
free of parcels, and looked back, searching for Mike. When she

saw him, she waved both arms. "So sorry," she seemed to be shouting. "So sorry." Her words were torn away by the wind.

Beside her at the rail the young English men and girls waved to the workers in farewell to their summer vacations. No one responded, but it didn't keep them from waving. Mike watched the ship until it was small on the horizon, then turned into the café.

It was his third day here. He was beginning to feel like an habitué of the dank little place, even if none of the cardplayers paid him any attention. Not that it was a café he would normally have chosen to frequent. Two days ago he had spent an entire morning walking the waterfront, carefully watching where the fishermen and dockers went for their drinks. At last he had followed them here. Alone among the waterfront cafés, it made no bid for tourist custom. There was not so much as a sign on its exterior; the pungent smell of wine, garlic, fish, and zinc that assailed the passers-by would have made one gratuitous. The noise of the bar ceased when he entered. He was the only patron wearing either coat or tie. He asked for wine and sat at a table near the door. The surly barman took his order and served him without speaking. For three hours Mike read Thackeray as he sipped the rough red wine, then left with as little notice taken of his departure as there had been of his entrance.

The second day he had come in shirtsleeves, and the barman had spoken in recognition. Today he was wearing the same shirt, now considerably dirtier, and he hadn't shaved. He went directly to the marble table where he had sat the two previous days, occupying the same straight, uncomfortable chair. When he ordered his wine, the barman said in a voice that was almost friendly, "A fine day, monsieur. Better than yesterday, isn't it?" Two of the regular customers nodded to him. Perhaps this was the day to speak.

Mike left his book closed. Behind the bar hung a cage with a silent pair of canaries. Probably they had given up singing in the face of competition from the shrill squawks of the gulls that swooped up and down in front of the café.

The barman put down the wine. "Monsieur is not going to England?"

Mike looked up. "Perhaps. How long does the steamer take?"

"One and a half hours. A good ship. It's French."

"Yes, it looks like a good ship. But I don't like big ships."

The barman considered him. "No, some persons don't."

"I wish," said Mike, then stopped and knocked the ashes off his cigarette. "I wish I could go by small boat. Maybe a fishing boat."

The barman made no answer, but picked up the ashtray and wiped under it with a filthy wet cloth. He flicked at a chair, looked around at the other customers, then picked up his tray, and started back to the bar. Halfway, he turned around and came back. "The fishing boats are busy by day, monsieur."

Mike nodded. "I know."

"They could go only at night."

"I know."

"Monsieur would not mind crossing by night?"

"No," Mike said slowly, "I'd prefer that."

"Well," was the only answer, and the man retreated behind the enormous coffee machine that stood on the bar.

Mike spent another hour or so in the café, but the barman did not renew the conversation, and at last he paid his bill and left. He wandered along the waterfront to the little restaurant where he had eaten his luncheon the day before. If anything could make the waiting tolerable, it was French food.

When he had eaten, he went back to the hotel. It was not too uncomfortable, but it was far from luxurious, and he was sure that he was the only English-speaking guest in the ten or twelve rooms that it contained. He picked up the heavy key at the desk and climbed two flights to his room. It was too much trouble to arrange for hot water in the middle of the day, so he contented himself with a shave in cold water. The pull of the razor was painful, but he felt better when he had finished, so much better that he gave himself a sponge bath in the cold water, then washed out his drip-dry shirt and underwear.

When he had finished his chores, he put on a pair of shorts and propped himself against the pillows of the bed before he lighted a cigarette. It had been years—in fact, nearly fifteen, when he was an undergraduate on his first summer tour of

Europe—since he had stayed in this kind of hotel. He lay looking over the foot of the brass bed at the big roses on the wallpaper, marching in faded splendor toward the neatly mended lace curtains at the window. Who was it who said that the French all had taste, and that most of it was bad? Fortunately, he didn't care too much about his surroundings, and with luck he might not have to stay here more than another night.

In Paris he had read all the English newspapers for three days, since the French and American press had only a brief squib or two about Jim. According to the English, the Russians in Moscow had admitted that he had flown there and asked for asylum. But it didn't make sense to Mike. The English authorities had been checking passenger lists and exit permits without finding any record of his departure.

It didn't make sense. Jim had been sympathetic to the Communists when he was an undergraduate, although he had never joined the Party. But that was nearly ten years ago, and he had recovered from his brief infatuation with Marxism long before graduation. Mike knew that. It might be hard to convince the authorities by saying that he knew Jim too well for the Russian stories to be true, but he was positive. All their lives he and Jim had been as close as two brothers could be, at least brothers who were four years apart in age. Jim had been totally frank about his political feelings when he was in college, and he had never bothered hiding anything from his older brother since then.

Furthermore, no man who had just become engaged was going to leave his fiancée in the lurch and volunteer to spend the rest of his life behind the Iron Curtain. Everything that Jim had written about Angela indicated that she was from a conventional background, and that she had never been sufficiently unhappy with her origins to revolt against them. "Conventional" had not been Jim's word; he had said something like "standard upper middle-class." But whatever the phrase, she sounded an unlikely person to go off to Russia, even to join Jim. It simply didn't make sense.

Mike watched the smoke rings drifting toward the lace curtains as he lay revolving the same old arguments that he had been going over for nearly a week. The clincher, of course, was the letter that he had in his jacket pocket. He kept coming back to the conclusion that he had originally reached in Paris: the key to Jim's flight to Russia surely lay in Market Doddington. Something must have gone wrong in the lab. Was there any way in which Jim could have been blackmailed into going to Russia? Not that he could imagine. Jim was a tough young man. Surely, only something that involved Angela could have meant enough to him to be the occasion for blackmail.

In spite of the Immigration authorities, he had to help Jim, and the first step was to get to Market Doddington.

As he reached over to stub the cigarette out in the ashtray, there was a knock at the door. He jumped to his feet and pulled on his robe. "Entrez." The door opened and a small, dark man came in. He was at least sixty, with an unshaven face, wearing dirty clothes that wafted the smell of fish into the room, but there was a twinkle in his eye.

"You wanted to see me, monsieur?"

Mike studied him for a moment, then waved to the single chair. "Sit down. What did you think I wanted to see you about?"

His visitor pulled out a crumpled pack of cigarettes and proffered it. Mike started to say that he had just finished one, then reached for the cigarette. He took his lighter from the bedside table and lit both the older man's and his own. Neither said anything. At last Mike spoke. "Who said I wanted to see you?"

"Pierre in the café."

"Are you a fisherman?"

The Frenchman shrugged. "Usually. But sometimes I take people out in my boat. It's expensive."

"How much?"

"That depends upon how long the trip is. Where do you want to go?"

"England."

In answer the Frenchman took a piece of paper from his pocket and wrote on it. He flipped it to Mike, who whistled as he looked at it. At a quick calculation of the conversion from francs, he knew that it was a little over one hundred and fifty dollars. "I haven't got that much in francs. Could I pay part of it in sterling?"

"Why not?" The man shrugged again, exaggeratedly, as if determined to look like a comic-strip Frenchman. "I'll have to take you at night. I'm busy fishing in the daytime. All right?"

"Fine. I guess we'll have to dispense with going through Customs if we go at night, won't we?"

His visitor looked disdainfully at Mike, as if the elaborate ritual of advance toward each other were both childish and silly. "That's the reason for the price. It's more dangerous for me than it is for you. If I'm caught, I lose my boat, as well as everything else. You can pay me half of it now and the rest tonight."

Mike was not good at accents in French, but there was something in the voice of the other that suggested it was not his normal language. "Are you French?"

"Breton" was the laconic answer. "Half of it now."

"How do I know I'll ever see you again, if I pay you now?"

"You don't."

It had taken so long to make this simple contact that Mike was willing to chance his money. He counted it out and handed it over. The Breton took it without looking and tucked it into a pocket. "Meet me tonight at eleven-thirty in Pierre's café. Bring your luggage, but put it behind the bar. Tell Pierre it's for Jean-Marie; he'll understand." He stood up and nodded. "Au revoir." In a moment he was gone.

Though it was more than eight hours before he was to be in the café, Mike found trouble in keeping himself from getting ready at once. Had it not been for the wet shirt and underwear slowly dripping over the washbasin, he would certainly have begun packing. As it was, he was forced to lie back down on the bed, and after a half hour he fell asleep.

It was after six when he woke up. Probably he would get little sleep that night, so it was good to have the nap under his belt. A sea breeze had forced itself through the curtains and flapped his little laundry dry. Half an hour later he was washed, dressed, and packed. Carrying his case, he went to the desk and explained that he was leaving. The manager's wife insisted on payment for an extra night, since he had given no notice of his departure.

Paying his bill brought his supply of francs near exhaustion. There would be enough for a good dinner and several drinks, but not much more. When he got to England, he would be all right for a long time, since almost his last act in Paris had been to go to the American Express office and change a thousand dollars into pound notes that he now wore in a money belt under his clothing. It seemed like an enormous sum, but if he were to move about under an assumed name, it would be foolish to cash any of his traveler's checks. Better to have too much money than too little. It was forbidden to take that much sterling into Great Britain, but it seemed a small illegality to a man planning to enter the country without permit.

The breeze that had dried his shirt was blowing freshly as he stepped out of the hotel with his suitcase. It was welcome after the heat of the past few days, but it might make the crossing more uncomfortable. From the quayside street the sea looked calm; it was hard to guess what it might be like a few miles offshore. At least he had thought to buy pills for seasickness in Paris. He was a good sailor, and he had been up and down the eastern coast of the United States in small boats, but even years of experience might not be of any help to his stomach if there were a stiff breeze in the English Channel.

A broad street ran from the quays to the main square of the town, seeming to connect two alien cultures: the land of the farmers and tradesmen, provincial and inward-looking like the inhabitants of any other small French town, and the world of the port, dirtier, busier, more invigorating, its only horizons those of the open sea. Most of the tourists who passed through the town came to wait for a Channel steamer or to find the nearest way to the railway station, and they seldom penetrated to the square, the heart of the provincial life, where in truth they would have been more at home than they were among the fishermen, the sailors, the dock workers, and the sleazy cafés and brothels on the quay.

Along the wide street, halfway to the square, was a sidewalk café where he had eaten the previous night. Its position

amused him, for it seemed a last bastion of the bourgeoisie overlooking the richer life of the docks. He bought a newspaper and
sat at one of the sidewalk tables.

When his vermouth arrived, he opened the paper and looked
unsuccessfully for a mention of Jim's name; the small stir that
the affair had created in France had died away, at least in this
coastal town. After a casual look at the headlines, he folded
the paper and lighted a cigarette, settling down to watch the
passers-by. Even at this distance from the water, the evening
seemed alive with gulls, swooping, screaming, quarreling over
bits of food in the street, making the gusty air hideous with
their noise.

There were other tourists sitting in the café. Mostly English,
he guessed, on their way home. With only fifty pounds to spend
abroad, the majority of them could not have been away more
than two or three weeks, but the difference in the looks of those
who were arriving on the Continent and those who were going
back to England was enormous. It wasn't simply the faces of the
latter, red with unaccustomed sun, or the fact that so many of
them wore espadrilles or straw hats, or even the bare legs of the
women and the open shirts of the men, forced into comfort by
Continental heat. It wasn't the string bags that they carried,
crammed with duty-free liquor and toys for the children. It was,
rather, their air of refusing to give up their holidays without a
struggle. One last Pernod, final orders of *vin ordinaire,* desperate
pilings-together of the remaining francs to see whether the total
would be equal to a box of chocolates for Mum in Walthamstow,
even the suspicion that every man was down to the last clean
shirt in his luggage. Vacations made one greedy to fill each
last moment. And all that Mike wanted was to get moving, to
leave France behind.

At the grocery across the street there was a small queue
of women waiting to finish their day's shopping before hurrying
home to prepare supper, their faces grim with haste. Beside
the grocery was a newspaper shop, before which a solitary man
with baggy English shorts and sunburnt legs leaned forward to
read the headlines, his back to Mike. A nun in short skirts flashed
past the café on a motorbike, her machine adding to the uproar

made by the other cyclists in the stream pouring back to the older part of the city from the docks. And, even above the noise of motorbikes, the screams of the gulls. Suddenly Mike felt very much alone, alien in an incomprehensible land. Perhaps that was the feeling that Jim had referred to in his letter. There was no one in the entire port to whom Mike could have turned in an emergency. Probably even his normally good French would desert him at such a time. He shivered slightly and took another drink of vermouth.

As he set the glass down again, he lifted his head and saw the man in shorts at the newspaper shop turn around briefly. For a moment their eyes met, then the Englishman turned his head away without response or recognition. Even as he turned, Mike was raising his hand in a wave, but it went unseen. "Mr. Stevenson, Mr. Stevenson!" he called. But the Englishman turned unhurriedly and began walking away down the street. Either he had not seen Mike in the moment when their eyes met, or he had not recognized him.

"Mr. Stevenson!" What his seatmate on the transatlantic plane would be doing in this most minor of Channel ports did not occur to him at first, but he was sure it was Stevenson. At least he was someone with whom Mike could eat dinner and with whom he could speak English. Stevenson had been pleasant, even kind, and if he was not much more than that, at least he would be a companion for an hour or two.

But Stevenson was walking away. Mike motioned to the waiter, who only flicked his cloth in recognition of the signal and continued his conversation at another table. Mike motioned again, but the waiter paid no further attention. Down the street Stevenson stood hesitantly at a corner, then turned left and vanished from view.

At last Mike dropped four francs onto the saucer beside his glass and raced down the street. It was too much, and he hated to overtip a waiter who had done so little for him, but Stevenson would have disappeared if he were to wait for the pleasure of the waiter. At the corner he stopped and looked along the street where he had seen Stevenson turn. It was wide, stretching ahead without another crossing for at least three hundred yards. Stevenson could not have reached a cross street in the thirty seconds or so since he had turned the corner. But he was nowhere to be seen.

After running down the street Mike felt silly that he had ever done so. It would have been embarrassing to come puffing up to Stevenson, shouting his name, when they scarcely knew each other. Better to let it go and eat alone. All the same he walked along the street looking into the shops. No Stevenson. Perhaps it had not even been his seatmate from the plane. Stevenson had been dressed in a business suit then, and Mike had probably made too much allowance for a change in his looks by the baggy shorts.

Feeling slightly ridiculous, he returned to the café and the inquiring looks of the waiter. After another vermouth he ordered dinner. Although he occasionally glanced at the street as he ate, he saw nothing more of the man he had taken for Stevenson. Anyway, there was no reason that Stevenson would be in this little port.

It was after nine when he finished his dinner. Slowly he went back to the bar where he had spent the three previous days. The barman made no comment as Mike handed him the case. "It's for Jean-Marie," he said. He settled down to wait for eleven-thirty.

CHAPTER THREE

FLORENCE EDWARDS settled into her chair, put her handbag on the deck beside her, furtively pulled down her girdle, and tucked her skirt in around her knees. It might be windy on the Channel. After a moment of indecision she tossed aside the steamer rug that had lain folded on the chair. It was hot, even on the shady side of the boat, and she could always pull up the rug if she got cold later on.

She had a new Deirdre Desiree novel to read, and that would help pass the time. *The Curse of Carnigham Court* it was called, and she knew that before she had finished two chapters she would be shivering in delicious terror at the troubles of a young woman caught in the toils of ancient malefaction in a moldering English country house. Deirdre Desiree was always dependable. Inexplicably, however, Mrs. Edwards found it difficult to begin reading.

She turned her attention to the young people standing at the rail of the ship as it began moving out of the little French port. Most of them were waving enthusiastically. She doubted that they really knew anyone to wave at, and decided that they were probably making exuberant farewells to a land in which they had been vacationing. But, even if they knew no one on the dockside, at least they had the pleasure of looking forward to being in their own country within an hour or two. Had she been at the rail, she would not have waved, for she felt sad at leaving France.

Determinedly she opened her book. "Her heart leaping in expectation, Penelope Fanshawe tried to preserve a calm exterior as the chauffeur said, 'This is the main entrance to Carnigham Court, miss,' and then turned the Daimler between great stone gateposts surmounted by weatherbeaten griffins." Yes, Deirdre Desiree was dependable.

After three chapters she tore herself away from the plight of Penelope, locked into the ancient central tower of Carnigham as the stable clock slowly struck midnight. Terror was no match for hunger, and Florence Edwards was not a woman to miss lunch lightly. She hoped that the boat ran to French rather than English cooking. Not that it could possibly be as good as the cuisine of Paris.

Paris, as it had turned out, was really quite different from Blandinsville, Illinois. Even more different than she had expected. Had it not been, she certainly would not have spent two full months there, the two months allotted originally to the whole Continent. She had not seen the mermaid in Copenhagen, or the manikin in Brussels, and St. Peter's remained only a name. But perhaps sometime she could make another European trip.

Of course, she had written to Alice Riggs explaining that she was staying in Paris to consolidate the French that she had so painstakingly learned with records in two years of correspondence course. But it wasn't true. She knew that she had remained out of love for a city, its people, and their ways.

The museums, for instance. Except for the Art Institute in Chicago, she had never seen a first-rate gallery before. But she had fallen in love with Renoir and Cézanne. Naturally, Renoir's models didn't look like real ladies, but there was an air of innocent abandon about them that she couldn't resist.

Or the food. It had seemed so rich at first, but now she was sad that she was leaving it behind. She would like to give Alice snails, the very idea of which had once been disgusting. After three weeks, she had timidly asked the chef in her hotel how they were prepared, and she had the recipe in her luggage. Probably she could order them from Marshall Field. They would be canned, but that might not make too much difference. And a bottle of Pouilly-Fuissé to go with them. She could get that sometime when she was in Peoria. She had never been inside the doors of the tavern in Blandinsville, and she was not about to start. Anyway, she doubted that it would run to Pouilly-Fuissé.

But it was really the Parisians who had won her heart. They were said to be cold and unfriendly. Perhaps they were with some people, but she loved them. Probably they had sensed her own shyness. In any case, they had been sweet to her. She would never forget Mme. Lenoir, with whom she had originally exchanged tips about knitting and who had wound up sharing with her the loneliness that widows know everywhere.

Whether she ought to tell Alice about the gentleman in the Champs Elysées was another matter. She had been looking in a shop window when she first noticed that the tall man with a handsome white mustache was attentively watching her. She had ignored him and started toward the Arc, trying not to show that she was aware that he was following her. She could have kept up the pretense if the walk had not been so crowded. At a crossing he had come close and pinched her—well, from behind her. His friendly fingers had encountered the nylon rigidity of her girdle, but she wasn't embarrassed.

She knew that she should have continued to ignore him, but somehow that seemed the wrong response when Paris was flooded with soft sunshine. On an impulse that she was sure she could never explain to Alice, she had turned and smiled. "Merci, monsieur." Before she knew quite how it had happened, they were walking arm in arm to a café for a grenadine. He was charming, and it had been such a long time—ten years, in fact—since Henry had had his coronary attack. At sixty it was probably safe to be a little indiscreet.

The following night they met for dinner at Fouquet's. She had been too shy before to enter the famous restaurant, where a lone woman would be conspicuous. It was different with a handsome man her own age. Over coffee he told her that he was married, so nothing more happened. Of course. Somehow, it had not seemed sad. Nothing more would have happened, even if he had been a widower. Surely it wouldn't have. But it was nice to have been noticed. And pinched.

She had no regrets, but she could not have put her hand on her heart and sworn that her two meetings with Paul had nothing to do with the fact that she had had her hair tinted a soft brown the following morning. It had been white, rinsed with blue, for so long that she was afraid the ladies of the Methodist Church would not approve. She would face Blandinsville when the time came, secure in the knowledge that she looked five years younger. She only hoped that it didn't make her look like a Renoir model.

She would have to get garlic in Peoria, too; there would be none in the grocery store at home. And garlic was an absolute necessity for snails.

After all, if she could show Alice her slides of the Renoirs, she could probably tell her about Paul. Alice was her own age, and though she had taught in the high school for forty years, she would probably understand. Even old maids must long for a comforting pinch occasionally. Yes, she would tell her, but it would be a good idea to slide over the fact that she had thanked Paul for his first gesture.

Anyway, it was all over now, and she was on the way to

England. Her reservations there had been made first, but she had deliberately set them for the end of the trip, in order to save the best for last. But now, after looking forward so long to the Tower and Stratford and the colleges—or was it universities? —at Oxford, it all seemed anticlimactic in prospect. At least, while she was there, she could send off the postcards for which there had never seemed to be time in Paris. Darn it all, tea would never replace Pernod. She sighed, put a finger in her book to keep her place, and looked around at the other passengers.

Perhaps it had been a mistake to come first class. She got up and looked over the rail at the tourist-class passengers. Most of them were young, far younger than she was when she had first been allowed to travel alone. She watched one group directly below her. Leaning against the bulkhead was a young man with a beard that had clearly not lived up to its owner's expectations, but its patchy spots didn't keep him from being singularly handsome in a pink-and-white way. He was sitting cross-legged, wearing nothing but dirty white shorts that showed off his deep tan. He strummed a guitar while he sang. The breeze blew his song away from her, but what she could catch convinced her that his fortune would never be won by his voice. Three girls and two other men lay on the deck around him in a circle, leaning on their elbows to watch him as he sang. The combined total of their clothing wasn't enough to make a dress that she would have considered decent when she was their age. How beautiful the young are, she thought, and how easily they respond to each other. It would have been pleasant to be near them on the crossing. Not to talk to them, but simply to enjoy being on the edge of their companionship. As the old woman in the red hat seemed to enjoy being near them and watching them.

It was time for lunch, but she hated to eat alone. On the tourist-class deck she saw a Frenchman and his wife eating sausages and bread that the man hacked from a loaf held close to his chest. A young English family were eating sandwiches and drinking tea made from a kettle perched precariously on a spirit burner that threatened to fall over with every pitch of the ship. One of the girls with the young man playing the guitar was unpacking food and passing around a wine bottle from which the others drank without even wiping its top. Most of the first-class passengers had already gone to the dining saloon. Only she was alone on the deck. And none of the tourist-class passengers was alone. None except the old woman in the red hat.

The red hat seemed to float on a mass of untidy gray hair. The old woman's face was streaked with furrows of sweat in runnels through the heavy layers of dust, but she seemed blissfully unaware of her appearance. A stout woman in tweeds unsuitably thick for the summer sun in which she sat. She was smoking a cigarette in a long holder, her fat legs sprawled out uncomfortably in front of her as she watched the guitar player. Clearly not a very nice type, as any of the ladies of the Methodist Church could have recognized at first glance. All the same, there was something appealing about the enthusiasm in her eyes.

Another glance around the first-class deck and the comfortable, empty chairs. It really would have been better to go tourist class, even if she had been advised that ladies traveling alone should always go first class. On a sudden impulse she went to the stairway—did they call it a ladder?—leading down past the young man and the guitar. The steel steps were treacherous as the ship moved gently up and down, but she negotiated them safely. In a moment she was standing before the old woman. "Excuse me," she began timidly.

The woman looked up. "Yes?" Incredible that she could have put into that monosyllable such a wealth of evidence of her Englishness. Perhaps it was the way in which she bellowed it, politely and incredulously all at once. "What can I do for you?"

"I wondered if—that is, are you traveling alone?"

"Quite by myself. Why?"

"So am I, and I thought you were. I wondered if you would like to have lunch with me." She gulped and hurried on before the old woman could answer. "I don't like to eat alone, and I seem to have done so a lot lately." The old woman hesitated; probably if she had to travel tourist class, she couldn't afford to patronize the ship's restaurant. "I mean, won't you be my guest?"

"How kind! What a splendid idea. I should be delighted." Her expansive gesture of gratitude knocked over a string bag holding several bottles. "Good heavens, I hope I haven't done anything to that cognac." She made an ineffectual effort to get to her chubby knees, then sank back down. "Why don't you have a drink with me first? The price they charge for drink on these boats is ruinous. It should be much cheaper than it is on shore because there is no duty, but it never is." She shook her head in chagrin at the cupidity of the world. "I always carry my own bottles. I hate to be cheated."

"Thank you, that would be nice." She didn't feel up to cognac before lunch, but she had to carry through, now that she had started. "I'm—that is, my name is Florence Edwards."

"How do you do. I'm Millicent Hetherege. English," she added gratuitously. "Is this your first visit to England?"

"It will be." She considered a moment, then lied gallantly, "I'm looking forward to it a lot."

"Good. Then let's drink to it. I hope you enjoy it as much as I enjoyed my visit to the States last year. I had a splendid time out there. What do you say to a little bourbon in your honor?" She rummaged among the assortment of bags around her and produced a flask and two plastic cups. No, the Methodist ladies would not have approved of her. Mrs. Edwards peered at her left hand; no ring. Not the way old maids ought to behave.

At lunch her companion ate so heartily that Mrs. Edwards was convinced that she must have been without food for days. Probably she had spent all her travel allowance on cognac to bring back to England. It was foolish to neglect food; that much she knew from Blandinsville. "Did you say that you had been to America?"

"Indeed I have. I spent five months out there last year. As a visiting professor at Wilton University. A splendid place. Wonderful people. My whole stay was somewhat disrupted by the murder of the chairman of the English department, but he was a bad man, I believe. I never met him. He was certainly a bad scholar. Never mind, I made a packet of money while I was there." She carefully licked the last of the chocolate mousse from her spoon. "Delicious! Do you know Wilton?"

Well, that settled it. At least she didn't have to worry about the poverty of Miss Hetherege, even if she had been unwise enough to spend all her travel allowance before she got onto the boat. "No, I've never been there. As an undergraduate I went to the University of Western Illinois, in Macomb. Actually, it was a teachers' college then. I had planned on teaching, but I got married instead. But that's a long time ago." And, if she was a professor, she was surely more respectable than her manner indicated.

"Ah, yes. Illinois. That's next to Pennsylvania, isn't it?"

On the paper napkin Mrs. Edwards drew a rough map of the midwestern United States, explained where Illinois was, and put in crosses to indicate the locations of Blandinsville and Macomb. Her new acquaintance watched attentively, and something about her face as she concentrated seemed familiar. She felt sure she had seen Miss Hetherege before.

"I live in a small town, too," she was saying. "Or, as we should say in England, a village. My brother and I have a house in Warwickshire, in Lower Doddington. He's an archaeologist, but he's retired now. And, since I've retired too, I spend about half the year there. I used to teach at Oxford, and I still have rooms at St. Agatha's, but I really prefer the country. He's lived there ever since his wife died."

"Oxford?" said Mrs. Edwards. "That must be nice. I'm hoping to go there in a week or two. I've always wanted to see it."

"It's lovely," Miss Hetherege answered. "I envy you your first visit there. Have you enjoyed France?"

"Oh, yes," was the fervent reply. "I'm afraid I didn't ever get outside of Paris, but I loved it. Have you been having a vacation in France? Isn't it wonderful?"

Miss Hetherege considered. "Yes, I suppose it is. I can't say that I approve of their politics, but they do make good wine and brandy. I've been at a conference of Arthurian scholars in Brittany."

Mrs. Edwards had put her handbag in a safe position beside the leg of her chair. She reached down for it when she saw the

waiter approaching with the bill. As she opened it to fish out
her purse, she caught sight of the back cover of the novel she
had been reading. On it was a photograph of the author, a
chubby, middle-aged woman; clearly it had not been taken
within recent memory, but there was no doubt of the identity of
Deirdre Desiree. Mrs. Edwards's favorite author was sitting
across the table from her.

She moved automatically as she paid the bill, her mind full
of the photograph on the book. With an absent smile she ac-
knowledged Miss Hetherege's thanks, almost unaware of what
she had said. She had never before met an author, and she was
not sure what she was supposed to say. It was particularly difficult because Deirdre Desiree had turned out to be a pseudonym.
Would it be rude to acknowledge that she knew who Miss
Hetherege was, or was it even less polite to ignore her identity?
It was difficult.

The most tactful way would surely be to give Miss Hetherege a chance to reveal the secret herself. As they walked back
to the open deck, Mrs. Edwards said, "I've just been reading
an interesting book, called *The Curse of Carnigham Court.* I
wonder if you know it?"

Miss Hetherege, who was busy lighting a cigarette in her long
holder, coughed on the smoke, spluttered, banged herself on an
ample chest with a hamlike hand, and finally subsided on a
deck chair. "Know it? Know it? Of course, I do." She looked
around in all directions with a rapidity that threatened the security of her red hat. No one was within ten yards of them. "I may
as well tell you, although I don't want it generally known. *I,*" and
she exhaled with pride, "*I* am Deirdre Desiree. Of course I know
the book. I wrote it." She swung her head back and forth again.
Apparently no spies had come to overhear her. "I'm *so* glad you
like *Carnigham Court.* I think it's rather good, too. Really, I'm
quite proud of it."

Florence Edwards had often read about the frequency of
shipboard romances, bred of propinquity and an enclosed area.
It had never before occurred to her that the deck of a ship was
as conducive to the growth of friendship as it was to more ro-
mantic intimacies. Nor, it had to be admitted, had her enthusiasm

for *The Curse of Carnigham Court* put any impediment in the
way of Miss Hetherege's response. Before the ship landed, she
had been invited to stay in Lower Doddington with the Hethereges, brother and sister, when she made her pilgrimage to
Stratford.

"Don't forget now," her new friend reminded her as they
parted at Victoria station. "We'll meet the train on Thursday. If
anything should prevent your coming, be sure to ring me up.
Here's a card."

Mrs. Edwards slipped it into her bag, and it was not until she
got to her hotel that she thought to look at it. "Dame Millicent
Hetherege, Cuthberts, Lower Doddington, Warwickshire. Tel:
Market Doddington 449." Even in Blandinsville she had read
enough English novels to know that "Dame" was a title. She
wasn't Miss Hetherege at all; she was Dame Millicent Hetherege.
Now she would never know what to call her. Could you just call
her "Dame"? Surely, that couldn't be right; it made her sound
like a character out of Damon Runyon. Or "Dame Millicent"?
That sounded equally awkward. There were times when she
longed for the simplicities of Blandinsville.

CHAPTER FOUR

Mike sat in the bow of the boat, the dark wind whipping at
his face and hair. It was more comfortable in the cabin, but the
smell of fish was overpowering inside. He didn't even know the
name of the other Breton, a man younger than Jean-Marie. He
had been waiting for them in the boat when Jean-Marie rowed
Mike out to it. It was a long way to row, for the boat was an-
chored some distance from shore, so that the noise of its engine
would not be so easily heard from the port. Mike had offered to
help, but Jean-Marie had refused, saying that he could row more
silently himself.

It had been hard to see much of the boat in the darkness, but it certainly gave no impression of trimness. That was the more surprising when Mike considered the speed with which they were moving; surely there was no reason for fishing boats to have engines either so powerful or so silent. Jean-Marie was probably used to this kind of nocturnal errand across the Channel.

In the distance Mike could see the intermittent flash of a light on what he presumed was the English coast. What was it Matthew Arnold had said? "The light gleams and is gone." But that was surely a flash from the French coast, not the other way around. It was impossible to judge distances at night, but they couldn't be far off England now. There were light fog patches hanging over the water, and the wind was cold, but the sky seemed clear. Deceptively clear, for he had not put on his raincoat when he first came outside, and now his jacket was wet, the tweed smelling like a rain-soaked spaniel when he moved his arms. He held up his palms to the wind, and within seconds they were damp. His hair would have been dripping were it not for the wind whipping it around.

Here he sat, getting wetter by the minute, while the two Bretons took turns warming themselves in the cabin. Right now Jean-Marie was inside, drinking coffee and brandy, while the younger man handled the boat. Alone again. Damn it, he was getting tired of being on his own. He had not spoken to anyone in simple friendship since he had left Mr. Stevenson on the plane. Nor did it look as if he were about to be rid of his loneliness soon. What he had to do, he had to do by himself.

He sat listening to the quiet, powerful throb of the engine. In a few minutes he would be in England, if all went well, the first leg of his journey accomplished. The only trouble was that he hadn't the slightest idea of what he would do once he was there. Of course he would go to Market Doddington, but then what? Then what, then what? The engine seemed to pick up the phrase, repeating it incessantly until it had no meaning. Then what, then what?

Gradually the engine seemed to distort the words, to change their monotonous rhythm with an irregular syncopation. Mike

felt a sudden giddiness, looking into the dark, his sense of hearing thrown off by the change of beat beneath him. Or was it
beneath him? The syncopation increased in loudness until it
almost drowned the original beat. Then he knew that it was not
a change in the rhythm of the engine of the boat. It was another
engine, and its sound came from in front of them.

He strained his eyes, but he could see nothing. The sound of
the engine increased, and over the noise he could hear the
monotonous dirge of a bell rocking back and forth on a buoy.
Presumably the Breton was standing behind the housing that
protected the wheel, so he would hear nothing over the sound of
his own engine. His own boat would not be seen, running without lights.

Slipping on the wet deck, Mike grabbed for the rail around
the wheel housing and pulled himself back to where he could
see the man at the wheel. "There's a boat ahead," he shouted into
his ear. "It hasn't got any lights, either."

The Breton only nodded, then said, "Get Jean-Marie." Without answering, Mike began groping a slippery way to the ladder
to the cabin. But before he could get that far, there was a brief
flash of light as Jean-Marie opened the cabin door. Mike knew
that the light in the cabin was dim, too faint to read by, but in
the thick blackness the sudden illumination was blinding. Perhaps because his sight was temporarily canceled, he was momentarily made doubly aware of sound, and the sound was that of
the engine of the other boat, paralyzingly, dangerously close.

As his eyes slowly adjusted again to the darkness, looming
above him he saw the vague shape of the other boat, also without lights, running as silently as their own in a deadly parallel
to their course. A mere flick of the wheel on either boat would
instantly close the gap of six or eight feet that separated them.
He could see neither Jean-Marie nor the other Breton, but he
knew that they must see their ghostly counterpart as well as he.
No two boats could run in such close formation without the
cooperation of both.

"Heave to!" The words were English, shouted but not through
the horn with which boats normally communicate. "Heave to!"
Mike doubted that either of the other two men on his boat could

speak English, but the import of the words must have been clear without definite comprehension of their individual meaning. For a split second a light from the second boat raked across Mike's face, and swung to the wheel, where he caught a brief glimpse of the two Bretons, neither looking at the other boat. "Heave to!"

In answer Mike felt the sudden swerve of the Breton's boat to starboard, and he had to grab quickly at the rails of the cabin ladder to keep from losing his balance. For a moment he felt as if he would never be upright again. The boat continued in a half circle and then he felt the surge of the engine even before he heard it, as the boat came out of its sickening lurch and straightened its course. Over his shoulder he could see the light from the coast, and the speed of the boat was so great that he could actually watch the light diminish in intensity and size. Obviously this was more than a mere fishing boat, and though he had been aware of the power of the engine, he had grossly underestimated it.

Almost as soon as the boat turned, he lost track of the sound of the other boat, drowned as it was by the sudden spurt of their own engine. Whether they were being followed or not he was unable to guess. Nothing broke the darkness, and his ears pounded with the pulse of the engine. The other boat was larger than theirs, and perhaps it was more powerful, but probably it would be less maneuverable.

When he was tired of straining his eyes for the other boat, he slowly worked himself forward to where Jean-Marie stood beside the other man. They had not heard his approach, and Jean-Marie jumped as he spoke into his ear, "What was that all about?"

Jean-Marie turned his head a fraction. "Get below."

Mike tried again. "Was it an English coastal patrol?"

"No. A coastal patrol would have turned its lights on." He gave Mike a push. "Now get below. It's dangerous up here."

He groped his way back to the ladder, then stopped before opening the cabin door. Jean-Marie had left the light on when he came out, and if he were to let it show as he entered, the other boat might see them. He could no longer see the English lights. At last he sat down on the steps and held on to the railing, against the constant swerving. After a quarter of an hour he felt the pulse of the engines diminish.

He stood up as Jean-Marie came to the head of the ladder. "Clever." There was admiration in Jean-Marie's voice. "They would have seen the light. But we can go in now." He leaned as the boat changed course again, then followed Mike into the cabin.

"What's up?" Mike asked.

"I don't know," was the sullen response. "Do you?"

Mike shook his head. "Why should I?"

"Why should you want to go to England?"

"That's got nothing to do with it."

"Possibly. Possibly not. I think we've lost them now. They didn't dare use their lights, and they would have had to turn off their own engines to follow us by sound. Do you still want to go to England?"

"What do you think? Of course I do. Let's go."

Jean-Marie shook his head in his turn. "We got away, but I'm not sure about losing them again, if they should hear us. They've got a big boat. Bigger than this one. I think we'd better turn back."

"Oh, no, we don't." Mike's voice was steady, though he felt nervous. "We go on. I paid, and I paid enough to take danger into account. How else could I get to England?"

Jean-Marie shrugged. "Perhaps the Channel steamer."

Mike cast around in his mind for some form of coercion that he could use. He certainly could not force two other men physically, and he could not threaten them with exposure when they returned to France. All that it would take to rid them of that threat would be a gentle heave-ho over the side of the boat, and he would never be missed. So far as he could think, the barman, Pierre, was the only person who knew that he had come out with Jean-Marie. And, if the boat returned without him, Pierre would assume—if he cared—that he had been delivered safely to the English coast.

He pulled out his wallet. Before leaving the hotel, he had transferred thirty pounds to it from his money belt. He held it out to Pierre, open so that he could see what it contained. "I'll give you all the money I have if you'll get me to England." He wasn't risking anything; if he went overboard, the money would do him no good.

There was a moment of silence, and Mike held his breath. At last Jean-Marie nodded slowly. "All right. We'll try." Mike hoped the other would not hear as he slowly exhaled. "You stay here." Jean-Marie stuffed the money into his pocket.

A minute or so after he had disappeared back up the ladder, Mike felt the boat change course again, and then the engine picked up speed once more. For nearly half an hour the boat tore along. Mike sat glumly, smelling the fishy aroma of the cabin. He could only hope that they were headed for England.

Jean-Marie stuck his head in the door. "All right. Bring your suitcase. It won't be long now." He disappeared again, and Mike followed him, carrying his bag.

Neither of the Bretons paid him any attention as he came up onto the deck. In a few minutes the engine slowed to a throb, then it was cut altogether. Jean-Marie pointed, and against the sky Mike could see what looked like a cliff, but he could not tell in the dark how close they were to it. "Where are we?" he asked. He was no longer even sure that it was the English coast. It would be a hell of a sell if he had paid all that money and then was dumped ashore somewhere on a desolate coast of France. "Where are we?"

"About twenty miles from Dover." The boat was still gliding forward, but with diminishing speed, now that the engine was switched off. When it had stopped, he turned back to Mike. "Here's where we drop you."

All that Mike could see was the water over the rail. "I can't swim with a suitcase. You'll have to get me in closer."

"You don't have to swim," Jean-Marie growled. He walked to the stern of the boat and began hauling in the painter of the dinghy. There was more decency in the man than he had expected, Mike reflected; at least he was going to row him ashore. When the dinghy was within reach, Jean-Marie leaned over the rail of the boat and picked up one of the oars. He handed it to Mike. "Here, you can see for yourself," he said. "Put it overboard, and you can see that it's shallow. You won't have to swim."

Mike leaned over with the oar. The water was not more than three or four feet deep. Deep enough to get wet, but he ought to be able to scrabble ashore. "Why don't you row me?"

"You may be pretty important, monsieur, if the other boat comes after you, but you're not important enough to me to row ashore. Over you go." Casually he picked up Mike's case and heaved it into the water. "Better hurry if that's worth anything to you."

"Go to hell, you bastard," said Mike in English as he dropped into the water. "I hope your boat springs a leak."

The water came to his waist, and it splashed higher than that, so that he was wet almost to his shoulders. But the footing in the sand was good, and he had soon waded the twenty feet of water that separated him from the shore.

The sand showed that he was in a cove, but aside from that he had no idea where he might be. The water streamed out of of his clothes as he walked across the sand. After about ten feet he came upon large rocks, and he could see the cliff directly above him. No use trying to climb that tonight. Out in the Channel he heard the muffled sound of the engine as the boat moved away from the shore.

He opened his suitcase and took out a change of clothes, thankful that they had not been soaked when the case was thrown into the water. He stripped, wiped himself as dry as he could with an undershirt, then dressed again in dry clothes. His wet things would not dry in the night air, but at least he could leave them out, since there was no use in getting everything else wet by putting them into the case.

His raincoat was wet, but it had not soaked up any water. He spread it out on the sand and lay down. "Then what?" The old refrain came back, but he put it out of his mind and went to sleep.

CHAPTER FIVE

Through the cold rain that fell unceasingly on the street, he could see the Olde Worlde tearoom crumpling in a most surprising manner; its carefully thatched roof dipped toward the ground, and the bow windows swam in circles, turning the women inside them like butter in a churn. Mike took a firm hold on the lamp post and closed his eyes. He would be feeling better in a moment. All he needed was a little rest. The big thing was not to walk too fast. Slow and steady was the ticket. He would have gone into the tearoom and sat down at one of the polished oak tables if he were not already awash with tea. He had spent three quarters of an hour drinking it in another restaurant, identical, so far as he could tell, with this one, except that it didn't have the distressing habit of turning itself upside down. He had dawdled at the table, contemplating the worm holes bored in Birmingham, trying not to see himself in the polished copper warming pans, concentrating on pulling himself together. What he really wanted was a drink, but it was another hour before the pubs would open their doors.

He opened his eyes. The women were still at their tea, which hadn't even slopped while they were spinning around. Stratford was bigger than he had remembered. And phonier. He could swear that the thatch on the tearoom was made of plastic. He looked at it again, but it began its old dizzying whirl, and he had to avert his eyes.

If it were opening time at the pubs, he could sink down in a corner and pull himself together while he decided what he had to do. Oh, God, if only he had bones in his legs instead of jelly. He knew now how a filleted fish felt. What would happen if he simply sat down in the middle of the sidewalk? Would anyone notice, or would they just step over him, as if it were New York?

He could close his eyes and let them use him as a hurdle. He wouldn't care. The hell with it.

But he knew that it was impossible. Whatever else, he had to keep from attracting any unnecessary attention. Otherwise, he could just go up to a policeman and say, "Look here, I'm in this country illegally, so why don't you arrest me and put me in a cell, where I can die quietly? Come on, pal, how about arresting me? How about it, huh?" Or he could go to a doctor or even a hospital. A nice hospital. A nice hospital with pillows and clean, dry, cool sheets that he could pull up over his face. A hospital would be a better place to die than a jail. They'd know what to do with the body. And he had Blue Cross. Ought to get some good out of that before he died.

He had felt pretty wobbly when he got off the train and put his bag in the Left Luggage office of the station, but he thought he could manage until he got a hotel. That was a joke. If there was an empty room in Stratford, he hadn't been able to find it in four hours of looking. Not that he blamed the reception clerks. Who would want to take in a guest who wobbled as if he were stoned, sagged at the knees, and leaned on the desk? If they had Alcoholics Anonymous in England, it was a wonder he hadn't been sent there, with a room booked for the next six months. It wouldn't have helped if he had said very quietly, very amicably, "Look, old buddy, I've got the flu, and I just want a place to leave this tired body when my soul takes wing."

Come on, Mike, cut the comedy. Let go the lamp post and get started down the street before the fuzz shows up. Head the old frame toward the railway station. If there isn't a train, maybe you can check yourself in Left Luggage. First the left foot, then the right. Chin up.

"Good afternoon. I didn't expect to see you here. I do hope I didn't hurt you."

He turned his head and tried to focus on the woman who stood before him. English, that was clear. But he didn't think he had seen her before. Gray hair under a red hat. Florid face. Maybe seventy, give or take a year. "Do I know you?" he began. "You've got the wrong man, I'm afraid." For a moment his memory tugged at the red hat. "Wrong man." The car in front of him began to stand on end, and he concentrated momentarily on the second woman. Brown hair, brown suit, sensible brown walking shoes. Camera. Younger than the other woman. Without warning the whole street buckled up into his face. "Just step over me," he murmured as the blackness took over.

It didn't stay black continuously, but he had trouble making sense of the faces that floated past. After a while he gave up trying.

He opened his right eye cautiously. Still pretty black. Not so bad as it had been, but black enough for any man. Left eye. That's better. Lots more light. But he still couldn't figure out the cloud hanging over his head. He closed his eyes again, and when he opened them, the cloud resolved itself into a tester over a four-poster bed. A night light burned on the table at the left side of the bed, leaving the rest of the room dim. Not bad for a police cell. Nice old polished furniture, chintz curtains that hadn't yet been drawn against the blackness outside, some glowing pieces of wood in the fireplace across the room. If this is police brutality, give me more. Pour it on.

A warder was knocking at the cell door. "Come in." Hard to recognize his own voice; all the stuffing knocked out of it.

However feeble he sounded, there was nothing weak about the response of the woman who barged in. "Good evening, Mr. Templeman," she boomed, and the Delft figures on the chimney piece shook. "How are you feeling? I thought I ought to poke up this fire. Can't have you freezing. Influenza chills are bad enough by themselves." She pulled the curtains and stumped stoutly toward the fireplace.

"I'm feeling better, but there's something we ought to get straight. My name's Church. Richard Church. I think you have me confused with someone else." He hoped it sounded more convincing to her than it did to him.

"Don't be ridiculous, Mr. Templeman," she answered without looking up from the wood she was putting on the fire. "I've seen your passport." She kicked the last log into place. "I must say, you're much handsomer without a mustache."

Frantically he put his hands under the blankets and felt his waist. The money belt was gone, and with it the passport concealed there.

"Don't worry about your money belt. It's in the top drawer of that chest."

"Look, let's get this straight. My name is Richard Church. Do you mind telling me who you are? And, if you don't think I'm being a Nosy Parker, I'd like to know where I am."

"You're beginning to sound irritated. That's a good sign. Influenza doesn't take long to recover from, but it's nice to hear you with so much spirit in your voice. Mind you, I don't see what you have to be irritated about. I told you about it all before."

"I don't remember," he said with the voice of a sulky small boy. "Tell me again." She stood up and looked at him full face. "Have we met somewhere? I seem to know your face."

"Very probably you do," she said noncommittally. "There must be thousands of people who know it. But we haven't met. Unless you count your getting in my way when I was running for the ship. My name is Millicent Hetherege."

"How do you do," he murmured, then felt abashed at his own conventionality. "My name is . . ." He stopped. The passport. "I guess you know who I am." There wasn't much point in denying it if she had already seen his picture. For what that was worth. He remembered the Immigration officer's remarks about it. Suddenly the meaning of what she had said struck him. "Great Scott, were you the woman with the bottles?"

"Of course." She looked faintly pained at the brevity of his memory. "A pity you got in my way."

Somehow the blame had been transferred, but he couldn't concentrate enough to figure out how it had happened. Besides, he was at a disadvantage. "How did I get here?"

"Mrs. Edwards and I had been at the afternoon performance and were just about to come home. When you toppled over, we bundled you into my motor and brought you here."

"Where's here?"

"Lower Doddington. About ten miles from Stratford. Where

did you think you were? Gaol?" He knew, without thinking, how she would spell "jail."

Before he could answer, there was a thunderous crash on the bedroom door, which had been standing ajar, and it flew open to admit an enormous yellow Labrador that raced for his bed and leaped up onto his feet, where it settled down at once for a nap. "Iseult! Get off there, you unspeakable beast." With astonishing alacrity Dame Millicent hauled the bitch off by her collar and dropped her on the hearth rug, where she yawned comfortably before falling asleep again. "Sorry about that animal. She's still a puppy in spite of her size."

Hoping to keep away from a discussion of jail, Mike put a hand out of the covers in the direction of Iseult. "I don't mind dogs. Don"t worry about me."

"Mr. Templeman, you look well enough to me to talk, so let's cut the cackle. Why are you here?"

"Well, you know, the standard reasons. I've always wanted to see Stratford." He swallowed. "I thought it was very pretty before I passed out."

Dame Millicent pulled an outsize cigarette holder from her pocket with one hand, while she rummaged around on the chimney piece for cigarettes and matches. "Smoke?"

Mike grimaced inadvertently. "I don't think I feel up to it yet. But go ahead."

His hostess sat down in one of the armchairs. "You look like an intelligent man, so why don't you stop wasting my time? First of all, only an idiot could think that Stratford was interesting. Second, you pretend that your name is not Templeman in spite of all the evidence to the contrary. Third, James Templeman disappeared from Market Doddington last week, and you turn up in Stratford this week." She took a puff from her cigarette and ran a heavy shoe over the sleeping back of Iseult, then looked directly at Mike. "Now, tell me why I shouldn't pick up the telephone and report you to the authorities. Mind you. I'm not particularly anxious to do so, but I want to hear your reasons why I shouldn't. I've been waiting until you were feeling better before I took any action."

"Well," said Mike, stalling for time, "there isn't anything illegal about my being in Stratford, even if you don't think much of it. And if, as you say, someone with the name of Templeman disappeared in the past, that still doesn't make it an offense for me to be here. I don't know why you are talking about phoning the authorities."

With a swiftness belied by her age and weight, Dame Millicent got to her feet. Iseult woke up and looked wonderingly at her. "Very well, Mr. Templeman, if that's all you have to say, I think we don't have anything more to talk about. I'll call the police now. You are quite welcome to stay here, if you have their permission, until you are feeling better, but I think you and I need not waste our time any further. Come, Iseult." She went to the door and took hold of the handle. "After all, I did see your passport. There is no record of your having entered this country legally. Perhaps you did, but you can explain that to the proper authorities."

She was half out of the door before Mike answered. "Wait, please. You're right, of course. Please come back." He watched as she hesitated, then slowly turned and sat down in the armchair again. Perhaps there wasn't much to be lost by telling her the truth; he was too weak, too tired, to think of a good alternative story to account for his presence in Warwickshire. If he let her go, she would call the police, and the best that could happen to him would be that he would be put on a plane for New York. The worst was that he might be treated as a criminal, tried, and sentenced for breaking the immigration laws. How serious his offense was, he had no way of knowing, but he doubted that the British took illegal entry lightly. Whatever the outcome, in that case, he would be able to do nothing for Jim. This old woman had already given him shelter when she realized that he was in the country without the permission of the authorities. That showed that she wasn't badly disposed toward him. Perhaps, if she knew the truth, she would even help him. "That's better. I'll tell you about it."

To his surprise her eyes lighted up as he told about his being refused entry at London, she beamed as he described his stay in the Channel port, and she got up, as if the suspense were unbearable, and took several steps around the room, brandishing her arms in the air, as he recounted the trip in the fishing boat. "Smashing!" she breathed when he told of the chase by the other boat. "How I do wish I had been there! Now, what do you suppose they were up to? Clearly, as your Breton friend said, they couldn't be anyone official; not our way, not at all English, to go around without lights. I'm sure they were smugglers; probably narcotics." She checked herself. "But do go on."

"It wasn't very heroic, I suppose, after that, to catch a cold from sleeping on a wet raincoat. But that's what I did. And it changed to flu when I was in London."

Her expression turned to disappointment. "Do you mean to say that you had no adventures going from the coast to London?"

"None, I'm afraid, unless you can count a journey by bus and British Railways as adventure. No one saw me in the morning; not so much as a barking dog took any notice of me."

"And then Stratford?"

He nodded. "Anticlimactic, isn't it? Sorry I can't do better for you. It's a little late for thanks, but I do appreciate your having taken me in. Does anyone else know who I am?"

"My brother, naturally."

"Your brother?"

"Surely, Mr. Templeman, you didn't think that *I* had undressed and bathed you. Or did you?"

"I hadn't thought about it, to tell the truth."

"Peregrine took care of you when we got home. When he found your money belt, he called me, and that's when I found out who you were. And Mrs. Edwards knows who you are, of course." She ticked off their names on her fingers. "But that's only three of us, so you needn't worry about your secret's becoming public property. If you're up to it, you may as well meet the others." She leaned around the wing of her armchair toward the open door. "PEREGRINE! FLORENCE!" Iseult stirred uneasily in her sleep, ears twitching, as Mike wondered whether the bellow could be heard in Stratford. Maybe Oxford. "FLOR . . ."

"Here I am," said a quiet Midwestern voice. Mrs. Edwards still wore the skirt of yesterday's costume, but she had taken off the jacket. Over her crush-proof traveling blouse she wore an outsize woolly cardigan. "How are you feeling, Mr. Templeman?" She turned to Dame Millicent. "I saw your brother start down the lane a few minutes ago."

"I'm afraid he's occasionally a little vague," Dame Millicent explained. "He starts out on errands and forgets where he is going." She caught sight of Mike's chagrin. "But don't worry about that. He's a gentleman, of course, and he wouldn't dream of telling what he ought not. It's only that he's forgetful, not indiscreet."

"You must be terribly worried about your own brother." Mrs. Edwards looked sympathetic, then flushed slightly.

Before Mike could answer, Dame Millicent spoke. "Florence, you aren't much of a conspirator. I'm afraid, Mr. Templeman, that I had asked her to—well, to be sitting outside the door while you and I were talking. You probably wouldn't have talked if there had been two of us in here, and she had to know in any case."

Whether he was simply weak from the flu, Mike could not have said, but he felt that command of the situation had long since slipped from his hands. All that he could do was to say, "Oh?" in a tone that he hoped would elicit an explanation of why Mrs. Edwards had to be privy to his situation.

"You see, Mr. Templeman, Dame Millicent and I thought it would be best if you didn't use your real name while you are staying here. No one would think anything of it if you were introduced as my son. We are both American and about the right ages to be mother and son. Would you mind?"

"I'd be flattered to be thought your son," he answered gallantly, "but I'm afraid I'm still a little behind the pair of you. Why the masquerade?"

Dame Millicent stirred impatiently. "Oh, come, Mr. Templeman. You don't think you'd get anywhere poking about in the neighborhood if you were to use your right name, do you? In any case, the police would be down on you at once if you did. Surely the local police would get in touch with their superiors if they thought you were related to the man who disappeared, and their superiors would no doubt know that you had been denied entry to the country. No, it wouldn't do."

"So, you see, it really would be best for you to be introduced as my son. We had decided that last night." Mrs. Edwards looked as if she needed reassurance. "And Dame Millicent and Mr. Hetherege would be the perfect entry into the neighborhood for you."

"Last night?" he asked resignedly. "You mean it was all decided before you ever talked to me?"

"Oh, yes. This morning Dame Millicent sent out invitations for the party on Friday. I'm afraid I thought of your being my son. It *would* work, you know. You don't look a thing like the pictures of your brother. The only drawback is that you are from Connecticut and I am from Blandinsville, Illinois."

"We wouldn't have to tell anyone that, would we?"

"No, but even to English people we must sound very different." She looked for confirmation to Dame Millicent, who nodded vehemently. "But I think that isn't serious. Where did you go to college?"

"Harvard."

"That explains it, then. Going east is what corrupted your speech." Mike suppressed a grin. "If anyone asks where you live, tell them Connecticut and that you are a lawyer, as your passport says. And say that you went to Harvard. No use in telling any unnecessary lies if you can help it. Don't you agree?"

"Fair enough, I guess. Yes, I do agree." This time he let the grin show. "Okay, Mom."

"Thank you, Mike," Mrs. Edwards answered demurely. "Michael Edwards. It sounds a reasonable name."

"If you are finished with this touching familial scene, Florence, I think we ought to let Mr. Templeman—Michael, that is —get some sleep. He'll have to be well enough by Friday to appear at the party. And don't look inquiring about *that*. I'll explain in the morning."

CHAPTER SIX

O<small>H, YES, I LOVE ENGLAND.</small>" Florence Edwards smiled at Mr. Plymson as sweetly as she knew how. "I've never been here before, but my son has. He loves it, too." Over his shoulder she could see Peregrine—Mr. Hetherege, of course—pouring sherry into the glass held by a woman in a large flowered hat, his floppy mustache moving up and down as he talked. "You must meet Michael." Peregrine wasn't so handsome as Paul, but he did have a lot of—what was the word?—presence. There was something about a floppy brown mustache that was more endearing than a stiff, white French one. "He's a lawyer. He lives in Connecticut now." And though she had always insisted that Henry have his suits pressed regularly when he was alive, she could see that there was a kind of casual elegance about Peregrine's— Mr. Hetherege's—shapeless tweed with the leather binding on the sleeves.

Oh, dear, she must attend to business. "No, I haven't known Dame Millicent long, but she and Michael became friends when she was teaching in the States. It was sweet of her to ask us to stay with her. I think the English must be the most hospitable people in the world." It was true, too. All those lonely weeks in France. It was a shame that she had wasted so much time there when she might have been in England. Really, there was no comparison between the two countries. Not that Mr. Hetherege would ever dream of pinching a woman he saw on the street.

"My uncle was with one of the large oil companies at home." And so he had been, although his duties were confined to filling the tanks of the cars that pulled up to the sleepy gas station outside the local garage. "It must be fascinating work. Petroleum is surely the most international business there is."

"Our branch of Coronado in Market Doddington is concerned

solely with research, so probably we're less international than some of the other branches of the company. Production and sales, for instance." Mr. Plymson wasn't bad looking, either, although he was a completely different sort of Englishman. Taller than Mr. Hetherege and considerably heavier. And his accent more English, somehow. Pale blue eyes. He kept reminding her of the actor who used to play Dr. Watson to Basil Rathbone's Holmes. "We were very fortunate to get a beautiful place like Doddington Hall for the Centre. Great shame, I suppose, that the old families have to give up their places, but I think that business has done a splendid job in this country in taking over so many of them. We had to turn it out from top to bottom, of course. No central heating, and the plumbing was appalling. We took out a lot of the old gardens, too. Shocking waste of time and labor for the sake of a few depressed flowers. No return on capital."

"Dame Millicent has told me that you've made it very beautiful." She crossed her fingers in the folds of her skirt. What Millicent had said about his taste hardly bore repetition to the director of the Research Centre; a few unimportant falsehoods did make social relationships easier. She took a sip of her sherry. Funny how she could scarcely remember the taste of Pernod. Or even grenadine, for that matter. "I don't suppose Doddington Hall is ever open to the public, is it?"

"Yes, one week in August, during the staff holidays. Swarms of people come to see it. Most of them want to see the Grinling Gibbons room. We normally use that for meetings, so we didn't have to make any important changes in it."

She sighed. "Oh, you make my mouth water. I love his work." At the moment she couldn't remember whether he was an architect or a painter, but "work" seemed to cover any eventuality. "But I'm afraid I'll not have a chance to see it. We'll be gone by August." She smiled directly into his eyes. She was glad that she had had her hair touched up in Stratford. Nigel Bruce! that was the name of the actor of whom he reminded her. How could she have forgotten? Peregrine, on the other hand, looked more like Ronald Colman. A pity that the movies didn't have the sort of faces they used to have. "It doesn't really matter, though. I suppose, with all the country houses in England, there must be more exciting rooms for me to see in other places."

The twenty or so guests hardly populated the long yellow drawing room of Cuthberts. The pretty Georgian house had not been at all what she anticipated. Somehow she had assumed that the Hethereges would live in a drafty farmhouse, smelling slightly of pigs and leather. But there was old chintz instead of leather, and the smell was of beeswax, potpourri, and the last of the lilacs from the garden, now drooping over the edges of a silver wine cooler. In Blandinsville Cuthberts would have seemed a big house, but it was small compared to the palaces she had seen in *Country Life*. By now it was probably stifling in Blandinsville.

Mr. Plymson looked annoyed. "I suppose the Gibbons work at Petworth is much better known, and it's more extensive, but the experts think that Market Doddington is considerably more refined. Not that I set myself up as an expert, but I do know a thing or two about Gibbons." She nodded doubtful assent. "Perhaps you would like to come and see it on Monday. I'd be pleased to show you around."

"That would be nice, but I'd not like to bother you. After all, I am going to Petworth, and I'd hate to put you to any trouble." Before Monday she had better find out what Petworth was, as well as the identity of—of—goodness, she had already forgotten the ridiculous name. Gribble? Gittings?

"Come for morning coffee. Afraid I can't ask you for lunch because I've got a meeting then. But do come at eleven if you can."

"That's very kind of you. I'll get Mike to bring me if Dame Millicent is busy." At the twitch of disappointment in his eyes, she brushed accidentally against him, and serenity returned to his face. She had forgotten how easy it was to flirt with a man in whom she wasn't really interested. There wasn't much scope for it in Blandinsville.

"You've probably heard about our American at Market Doddington?" At her look of bewilderment, he continued, "A chap who had been working for us in research. An out-and-out Bolshie. He took French leave a fortnight ago. Russian leave, actually; he went to Moscow. Real international scandal. However, no

question of that with you." He managed to touch her hand clum-
sily. "Or your son, of course. Incidentally, I see that he's talking
to the Woodhouse girl. She was engaged to our American. Left
her high and dry. But that's the sort of thing they do. A certain
kind of Yank, I mean, not your sort, dear lady."

Sixty, if she was a day, Mike thought. From some God for-
saken little place in the Midwest, on her first trip to Europe,
wearing a nylon blouse and sensible shoes, and she was carrying
on with the calm assurance of a woman half her age with a
world of experience. Women were wonderful. Not that she was
bad looking for sixty, or whatever she was, but she certainly wasn't
a beauty by any standards. At least, until she put her mind to it.
Mousy, he would have said, but she had the fish-faced director
breathing hard. Perhaps all it took was self-confidence. But the
old Blimp had better watch out or he'd have a heart attack. God
bless her, anyway. And she looked as if she were enjoying it.
She saw his glance and gave him a motherly wave.

He wished that he were as good as she at acting. Angela
Woodhouse seemed to be everything that Jim had said. Perhaps
not so pretty as he had imagined, but he could hardly expect
that from a girl whose fiancé had presumably left her without
a word a couple of weeks ago. Maybe if he were not still so
weak from the flu, he could manage to keep up a light line in
cocktail chatter. As it was, he found it the hardest conversation
he could ever remember. She looked so vulnerable that he
wanted to put his arm lightly around her and let her cry against
his shoulder. "She's a marvelous woman," he said. "I didn't get
to know her until she came to the States to teach. She's been
wonderful to Mother." But she didn't look the sort to cry easily.

"She holds this whole village together. She used to be away
a large part of the year in Oxford, but she would often come
down here at weekends. I suppose it comes naturally to her; her
family has always owned this house, although her parents were
hardly ever here. A lot of the villagers think she is an interfering
old busybody, but they all respect her, and they don't dare dis-
obey her when she makes her mind up."

"Sound fairly feudal to me. I thought that had gone out a
long time ago."

"There's nothing feudal about it at all. It's sheer force of personality. Only last year the daughter of the man who runs the village shop got pregnant by a boy who works at the garage in Market Doddington. He wasn't going to marry her. Not until Dame Millicent heard about it. She went straight to the garage where he was working. She marched into the garage, took the spanner out of his hand, and announced to him that he was going to take a walk with her. When they came back, he looked white and fairly well shaken up. A week later he had married the girl. That's what I mean."

"How did it work out?"

"Fine so far as anyone can tell. There's another baby on the way now." For the first time, she laughed. "I think that was his own idea, however. I doubt if Dame Millicent had anything to do with it."

"What do you do when you aren't coming to sherry parties here?" He felt a hypocrite asking, since Jim's letters had told him more details than she could fill in by a full day's talking.

"I work for a publisher in London during the week. Not very glamorous, I'm afraid. Mostly I read manuscripts of mysteries. That's about all they'll let a girl do the first few years. And make tea, of course. I hadn't realized how much tea we English really do drink until I went to work for Hayes and Brimsley. I usually come home for weekends. My parents have always lived here. Daddy's the local doctor. I got off early today, which is why I could manage the party. I often bring manuscripts home for the weekend, so they don't mind if I'm not there until five."

Her eyes were beginning to look more animated, and Mike could tell why Jim thought she was so pretty. But, even when she had laughed, there was still a crumpled edge to her voice that betrayed a deep substratum of grief. And there must be steel there, too. Otherwise, she could not have carried on working during the past two weeks, when her name had constantly been in the newspapers. He shied away from thinking of the pain she must have felt as she tried to read manuscript after manuscript of light-weight fiction.

"Who's the man talking to Mother? Do you know him?"

"Mr. Plymson. He's the director of a research center near here." She hesitated briefly, then went on. "He looks as if he were having a good time. I don't blame him. Your mother seemed charming when I met her. But I didn't have much time to talk to her. It's obvious that you are her son, isn't it?"

"You think we look alike?" was the best that he could manage.

"I didn't realize that Dame Millicent knew him. I've never seen him here before. But it's not surprising. She knows everyone." Either her voice betrayed a slight reserve about Plymson, or she was feeling natural reluctance to see the head of the concern from which Jim was thought to have stolen important data. Hard to guess which.

"Brace yourself. Here he comes with Mother. I imagine she is going to introduce us."

"Excuse me a moment. I must see Dame Millicent. I'll be back in a minute." Before Mrs. Edwards and her new conquest reached him, she was gone. That "Brace yourself" had been stupid; it seemed to suggest that he knew she wouldn't want to talk to Plymson. But it was too late now.

"Mr. Plymson, I want you to meet my son Michael."

Plymson held out his hand. "How do you do, Mr. Edwards."

"Darling, Mr. Plymson has asked us to have morning coffee with him on Monday to see the beautiful old house where he works."

Michael was a good-looking man, Dame Millicent thought as she watched their meeting. Two days ago he had been badly in need of a shave, and his color had been unimpressive, but rest and enforced draughts of whiskey seemed to have done him a lot of good. She had never met his brother, but Michael was handsomer than the pictures of James Templeman. And certainly far better looking than Douglas Plymson. To think that the day had come when she had actually invited the man into her house. She took a long pull at her drink for consolation.

Not a bad party, really, with the exception of Plymson. Dr. Woodhouse was always a pleasure, and his wife was good-hearted even if she was a trifle dim. The daughter seemed to be bearing up fairly well, too. She hadn't really expected her to come when she sent the invitation. Good stuff in the girl, however, and she might have known she would accept. It made it easier this way for Michael to meet her. Otherwise they'd have to lie in wait for her and pop out on the footpath. Or lurk for her after church. Hard luck for a man to have to meet his brother's fiancée that way. Michael seemed to be getting on well with her, all the same.

As she watched, Angela detached herself from Michael and came toward her. Perhaps they weren't getting on so well as she had thought.

"What a nice party, Dame Millicent."

"Thank you, my dear. I'm so glad you could come."

Angela smiled. Just a touch too bravely? "Not much sense in moping, I think." Bless her. "Actually, I wanted to ask you about Mrs. Edwards. I don't know what you have planned for tomorrow night, but I wondered whether she might like to go to the theatre at Stratford with me if you had nothing on. It's *Twelfth Night,* and I've got an extra ticket. I'm sorry I haven't got more, so that I could ask you all. I bought a pair several weeks ago for me and—well, I thought perhaps she would enjoy going. Most Americans seem to like Stratford, and perhaps she hasn't had a chance to see it yet. But I don't want to spoil any plans you might have."

Over Angela's head she could see Florence and Michael talking to the Plymson man. No wonder she had left Michael. "How kind of you." Good luck they had already seen the play. "But I'm afraid it's no good for Mrs. Edwards. She and I saw it the other day." She paused, as if feeling hesitant. "I don't suppose I should tell you this, but I do know that her son was terribly disappointed that he couldn't go. It was the day that he arrived, but he was so ill that he couldn't go with us. I tried to get another ticket for him when I returned the one that he couldn't use, but you know how difficult it is at this time of year. And he said that it was his favorite comedy, too. But perhaps he can pick up a ticket sometime. It *would* be a shame if he were to miss it." She hoped she wasn't too obvious.

If so, Angela chose to ignore the fact, although she frowned slightly before she spoke. "Perhaps he would like to go instead of his mother. But I don't quite know how to ask him. It might be awkward for him if he'd prefer not to."

"Perfectly easy, my dear. I'll ask him for you, and I'm sure he would be delighted." He'd better be. "If you could draw Mr. Plymson's fire for a moment, I'd ask him now." If Angela had the stuff to keep on living a normal life after what had happened, surely she could face up to talking to Plymson. Not that it would be a pleasure, but it would be much easier than what she had gone through in the last fortnight. "Let's join them."

A pleasant young man, Peregrine Hetherege was thinking, but, for the life of him, he couldn't remember who he was. Slightly shy, still pink and white like a schoolboy, and remarkably nice manners. That kind of manners had almost disappeared. Pleasure to see them. "Like some more sherry?"

"No, thank you. I've still got most of my glass."

"Good. I'll have some, too." He stepped to the table and picked up the decanter. Millicent was always giving these damned great parties. He was expected to be there, but she seldom bothered telling him about them until the guests were arriving. Probably because he had once dug in his heels and refused to come out of his room. Nowadays it seemed he had hardly turned his head before they were trooping in at the front door, cutting off his retreat up the stairs. And he'd be damned if he would use the back stairs out of sheer funk. Still, this wasn't as bad as most of her big bashes. "Here you are."

From somewhere the young man had managed to fill his glass while his back was turned. Not the sort of thing you'd expect from an apparently well-brought-up man. Still, times changed, and it was no use complaining. "Do you hunt?"

"I'm afraid I don't have much time these days. We've been particularly busy at the lab."

Sounded like a scientist fellow. Not that you'd have guessed it of him if he hadn't admitted it. "Where's your lab?"

"In Market Doddington."

"Of course, of course. I met someone else from there today."

"Mr. Plymson?"

"Don't remember his name. Could be Plymson, though."

"He's the Director of the Centre. Over there. With Miss Woodhouse." He pointed.

Angela was taking Plymson to the far end of the drawing room to see the Ruysdael hanging over the chimney piece, and Dame Millicent retailed her invitation to Mike. "It couldn't have worked out better, and if you don't know *Twelfth Night,* you'd better read it in bed tonight. I've said it was your favorite Shakespearean comedy, and it wouldn't do for you to be ignorant about it."

"Don't worry. I played Viola when I was in school. The hairiest legs in the history of the character, but I do know the play. I'll ask her to dinner beforehand."

Florence Edwards looked wonderingly at her hostess. "Somehow, there's a devious side to your character that I hadn't suspected."

Dame Millicent smiled complacently. "Devious is perhaps a bit strong, but I do think it is fair to say that I sometimes plan things well. How about another sherry? As a matter of fact, I'm not at all sure that I had to do much planning this time. I had a feeling that perhaps Angela was maneuvering me all the time. Besides, after your little success with the Plymson creature, I don't think that an accusation of deviousness comes very becomingly from you."

With wide eyes Florence replied, "Good heavens, I don't know what you mean. By the way, who *is* Gritling Gibson?"

CHAPTER SEVEN

HERE'S WHERE HE'S BURIED." Angela pointed. "I hope they never disturb his body. If it's still there."

Half aloud Mike read:

> "Good friend, for Jesu's sake forbear
> To dig the dust enclosed here.
> Blest be the man that spares these stones,
> And curst be he that moves my bones."

He looked up at the painted stone likeness. Somehow, it was all here, the contrast between the simplicity of the inscription and the encrustation of legend that gradually overlaid the bare stone, an encrustation that finally overwhelmed the reality and left little but a vulgar industry of prosperous Bardolatry. Not, God knows, that his was an original observation, but to stand by the still point of the inscription made any thinking man cast the thought anew. "It's enough to make you forgive the rest of the place, isn't it? Dame Millicent doesn't think much of Stratford, but I'm getting to like it. Well, part of it, at least. Remember how angry that woman was this afternoon?"

They had gone to the Information Centre to look at a map of the town. Mike had innocently asked the woman in charge how much of Stratford was genuine Elizabethan. "Are you from television?" she demanded.

"No, I'm just a tourist."

"Those television people are always coming around, trying to make out that it isn't all genuine. Are you sure you aren't from the BBC?" Her voice glinted with animosity.

Apparently his second disclaimer did not serve to allay her suspicions, for she had dragged them into a neighboring house. "There's an eighteenth-century front on this, but look at the beams. They are Elizabethan. Genuine Elizabethan, and if you know anything about architecture, you'll recognize them. But none of you people from television have the slightest inkling about authenticity. Always trying to belittle what you don't understand. It's genuine. The whole town is genuine."

Taking Angela by the elbow, Mike had slid toward the door, murmuring his thanks in counterpoint to her belligerent outpouring. Cries of "Genuine!" pursued them down the street. "Authentic!"

"Poor old dear. It really wasn't very tactful of you to ask

about the fakes. And I suppose she forgets about Hamlet's Hamburger Heaven." He was beginning by now not to be surprised by her smile.

Late-afternoon light was streaming in from the clerestory, and it was dim only under the great carved organ case where they stood. Most of the tourists were gone from the church now, and the blue-robed verger had few fees to collect for entrance to the chancel. An elderly workman was busy varnishing chairs, then upending them, so that they would not be sat upon until they were dry. The verger left his post to chat with the workman, and as he did so, four pretty, long-legged Scandinavian girls walked in without paying. He had hardly finished limping after them to collect two shillings from each before a woman entered, brandishing her stick: "I don't pay, my good man. I was christened and married in this church, and I am a friend of the Archdeacon."

"She's rather like an older Dame Millicent, isn't she?" Angela asked.

"At least the place seems to attract characters. Look at that pair. You wouldn't think they had ever been in a church before." Mike indicated two young men who wandered in, looking about them suspiciously. They were dressed almost alike in brand-new sports coats of regrettably flamboyant pattern. Although one was nearly six inches taller than the other and their features were unlike, they had an uncanny resemblance, perhaps because of the swelling muscles that strained both coats, and the incongruously pinched faces above opulent pectorals, sharp faces that looked as if they had been hungry in childhood. They tiptoed around the chancel, apparently afraid to repeat the clicking of their pointed shoes on the stone. "They're bookmakers, straight out of an English comedy film. I'm surprised they didn't try to gamble with the verger for the entrance fee."

Angela glanced at her watch. "If you've had enough culture, we probably ought to be going toward the theatre. They'll be serving dinner in another half hour. We needn't rush, and it's a pretty walk."

It had been a softly sunny day, but there was already a light mist hanging over the river. The hospitable gardens were full of people converging slowly on the big theatre. Young people in jeans and sandals mixed easily with their elders, dressed in felt hats and well-laced shoes. Two portly American men with watch chains over their swelling waistcoats walked directly ahead. "Visiting professors at the Shakespeare Institute," Angela hazarded.

A minute or two later Mike saw across the way the terrace of a pub, its chairs and walls full of young people with drinks in their hands. "What's that?"

"We've got time for the obligatory pint at the Dirty Duck, if you like." Without waiting for an answer Angela crossed the street and started up the steps, Mike in her wake.

"We'll never find a seat," he muttered, half to himself. But fate intervened, and Angela plopped down on the wall in the vacant space left by a departing couple. Most of the youngsters around them were conspicuously beautiful: the girls with heavy makeup, as if they had just run out for a drink between performances, the young men with carefully brushed hair that looked as if it had recently been released from a property helmet. "Are these actors from the theatre?" he asked.

Angela grinned. "Don't you believe it. Probably most of them came on a coach, but they would be delighted to be taken for actors."

Mike had to keep himself from staring at her. She was as pretty as Jim had said, and she was as charming. The only thing missing was any sense of close personal contact with others. Behind the charm there was a wall, effectively cutting him off without ever being offensive. It was hard to characterize. But perhaps it was lucky that it was there, all the same, or he might have been in danger of getting too interested in his brother's girl. And that, most distinctly, was not the purpose of the operation.

She seemed content not to talk as they drank their gins-and-tonic, looking over the street toward the river, with the honest-to-God Victorianism of the Picture Gallery filling the middle foreground. Stratford teemed with transients. Surely someone must live behind the half-timbered fronts of the houses lining the streets, but, if so, they were keeping themselves well at

home. Coaches from all over England wormed their balky way
down the narrow street, the occupants looking with envy at the
drinkers in the pub. California housewives and German students
in dirty leather shorts jostled each other on the pavement.

Putting her hand on his arm so suddenly that he almost
spilled his drink, Angela pointed at a mud-caked blue Vauxhall
in the slow queue of the street. "There go your bookmakers,"
she said. "They must have had enough of the parish church. You
don't think they are going to the performance tonight, do you?"
The taller of the two men was driving the car, his face a study
in sullen frustration as he waited for the traffic to move. Neither
of them looked up at the Dirty Duck. "I think they'd be a lot
happier with a pink gin."

Contrary to what Dame Millicent had said, *Twelfth Night*
was not Mike's favorite Shakespearean comedy. But the performance was good, and within a few minutes after the curtain
went up he had succumbed to the lyrical green-and-yellow
melancholy of Illyria. "Like it?" he whispered as Malvolio
puzzled over the letter, and Angela nodded, her smile shining
in the darkness. Today she seemed to have shed all the carefully
controlled grief that he had sensed yesterday at Dame Millicent's sherry party. Except for the high wall of which he was
so conscious, her manner might have been that of any nice girl
having a pleasant day with a man a little too old to be immediately exciting to her. Half of him was pleased that she
seemed less sad, half worried that she appeared almost to have
forgotten Jim. Or had she? He didn't really know her well
enough to be positive. It was much too early to try to bring up
the subject of Jim, even if he could think of a way. He forced
his attention back to the bantering of Viola and the clown.

During the interval, for the first time that day, he found it
difficult to think of things to talk about. Perhaps because he felt
obscurely hurt that she appeared not to be remembering Jim.
It was foolish, but he found himself worrying about what to call
her. When she had phoned to say that she was coming to pick
him up, she had begun the conversation with "Mr. Edwards."
Since then neither of them had used the other's name, and the
longer it was postponed, the harder he found it to say either

"Miss Woodhouse," which sounded stilted, or "Angela," which seemed to postulate more intimacy than she would welcome. "I'm glad Mother had already seen the performance," he said. "I'd hate to think I might have missed this."

"I'm delighted." Her tone was so perfunctory that he felt rebuffed. She seemed to be considering. "I can't get over how much you look like her. It's an amazing resemblance."

"Item, Two lips, indifferent red," he quoted. "Item, Two gray eyes, with lids to them; Item, One neck, one chin, and so forth." He forced a laugh. "Most people don't think I look like Mother." This was the second time she had remarked upon their likeness, but he knew perfectly well he didn't even accidentally resemble Mrs. Edwards. "Am not I consanguineous? Am I not of her blood?"

Angela cocked her head. "You've got a good memory."

"I told you I played Viola."

"Were you good at disguise?"

The bell rang, ending the interval and sparing him the necessity of replying. He wondered if Angela really thought he looked like Mrs. Edwards. If she were covertly commenting on their lack of resemblance, he couldn't see the point.

After the performance there was barely time for another drink before the pubs closed. "I know one a little distance from where I parked the car," Angela told him. "It's not so quainty-dainty as some of the others, but you've probably had enough of that for the day. Let's go there."

When they had their drinks, she held up her glass. "Cheers. Dame Millicent told me that you are a lawyer. From New York?"

"No, Connecticut. Greenwich. Have you ever heard of it?"

"Not of that Greenwich." She looked wryly at him. "Only of our imitation of it here in England. Tell me about yours."

He groaned. "It's impossible. Try to think of a mixture of Surbiton and Chelsea, with a dash of Sevenoaks, and then stir in a few spoonfuls of the country houses in Hertfordshire. When you've got it all put together, you won't have Greenwich, any more than I ever get the intended result with French recipes, but you'll at least have an idea of the fact that it is an exceedingly strange place. Snobbish, suffocatingly suburban without knowing it, elegant, and very plain indeed. I think I like the plain part best. If it weren't for that, I'd probably leave. That is, if I got a good offer from a law firm somewhere else."

"Is your family there?"

"Mother lives in Illinois, as you know. My former wife is in New York with her second husband. No children. My—my brother is abroad."

"My brother he is in Elysium." Angela had not lifted her eyes from her beer as she whispered the line. Without answering Viola's plaint, Mike switched the talk to his law practice. That was safer ground.

By the time the pub closed, chinks were becoming apparent in the wall he was so conscious of Angela's having reared. As they hesitated on the paving outside, before turning in the direction of her car, she took his arm, looked him directly in the eye and said slowly, "I do feel very much at home with you."

In another woman it would have been a straightforward declaration of interest, and he chose to treat it as one, even if he didn't believe in it. "And I with you. Tell me about yourself. You've kept me talking constantly. What's your life like? Are there lots of men in it?"

Still holding his arm, she looked down the street, turning her head from him. "I think a left turn down here, along Blunt Lane, is the quickest way back to the car. No, there aren't lots of men. There's only one. And he's abroad. I hope that Dame Millicent will take you to Ragley Hall sometime. You'll like it, I think." And that was as much as she seemed inclined to say about her emotional life. Another time, and perhaps she would begin to talk about Jim. But it was probably too much to think that she would confide anything very telling about him to a comparative stranger.

Blunt Lane was a long, narrow passageway, with small houses on the right side, overlooking it across diminutive gardens and an inadequate stone pavement for pedestrians. On the left the street was entirely blanked out by a wall running its length. It appeared to be the wall common to several gardens, for at intervals it switched heights and changed from stone to brick and then back again. Blank it was, for there were no doors, but it was not unfriendly. The street lamp that projected from its surface halfway down its length revealed wallflowers growing in the chinks, their lingering odor powerful in the night air.

Angela's arm was still in his, and the pavement was too narrow to walk abreast. Talking quietly in the hush that settled over them as they entered the lane, they made their way down its central depression, taking care not to turn ankles on the irregular stones. "Now I know something," said Mike. "This is where the people of Stratford live, not in all those half-timbered places we saw. Real, live people with children and bunions, worrying about income tax and weeds in the campanula. This is what I've been looking for."

The street lay mainly dark under the luminosity of the late-evening sky, although an upstairs light or two showed behind closed curtains. A thin stream of wiry melody forced itself through an open window. He listened. "The *Grosse Fuge*. Not my idea of bedtime music."

"Really rather good, I think." They were nearing the far end of the lane. Under the street light Mike saw a late walker cross the corner. Angela stopped before the turning to hear the end of a phrase. "By the time that whole marvelous fugue had been unraveled, I'd be unraveled too, and ready for sleep."

Beethoven was overwhelmed by the incursion of a car motor on the cross street, approaching the corner. The acceleration of sound indicated the speed at which the car must be traveling, but no lights shone on the street ahead. "Silly damned fool to be driving without his headlights," Mike growled, then fell silent at the noise of brakes hastily applied.

In the light of the corner street lamp he saw the car turn sharply left, headed down Blunt Lane. The tires squealed as the car went over the curbing, narrowly missing the lamp post. Angela suppressed a scream and jumped for the safety of the pavement. Mike, close behind her, seized her waist and heaved her forward, throwing her over the low garden wall in front of the nearest house. Tires still wailing, the car swerved, almost hitting the high wall on the other side of the street, then headed straight for Mike, and, as it approached, its lights switched to full blinding blaze. With a primordial grunt Mike instinctively leapt forward.

His jump did not carry him quite out of range of the car, and its side caught him on the shoulder, hurling him still farther forward. He turned in midair and hit the pavement with the same shoulder, then rolled over two or three times before coming to painful rest. Behind him he heard the grinding of metal as the car grazed the wall toward which he had heaved Angela, then the racing of the engine as it lurched off the footpath and picked up speed. Groaning, he rolled over and tried to see the license number. As he looked, the lights were extinguished on the car, but before they went out, he was able to see that the license plate was covered with mud that made the number indecipherable.

An unshaded light knifed out of the darkness from the front door of the house nearest him. "Angela!" he called. "Angela!" Lights sprang on up and down the street. He began pulling himself to his feet.

"Mike, Mike! Are you all right?" Suddenly the street was full of people, some in dressing gowns, some still in pajamas, one man wearing nothing but a scanty pair of briefs. In the now more-than-adequate light, he saw Angela climbing back over the wall toward him, her stockings and dress torn, her hair disheveled. "Mike. Oh, thank God." Slowly she slid down into a heap on the street, but she had not fainted. She simply sat there, her legs thrust out awkwardly, quietly sobbing. In the background, undaunted, the *Grosse Fuge* continued its logical, gloriously unpredictable course.

"What the hell do you think you're doing?" The man in briefs stood over him, so close that Mike had to move aside to stand erect. "What's going on here?"

"A car came up onto the sidewalk and nearly hit us." And the hell with you, too, mister.

"You damned Yanks, always causing trouble," the man said balefully.

"OH, SHUT UP!" The startling noise came from Angela, glowering up at the angry householder. "Shut your bloody mouth. Can't you see that we were nearly killed? Don't just stand there blathering in your silly underwear. Help him to stand up, you bloody fool. And SHUT UP!"

Dismayed, the man looked down, saw his briefs agape, covered himself with an insufficient hand, and scuttled for the shelter of his own house. "Don't worry," Mike called, "I'm all right." He limped towards Angela. "How are you?"

"Furious. I've torn my stockings and skinned my knees, but otherwise I'm fine. That is, I think I am. I feel a little weak in the knees, but I don't think it's because they're skinned. I've never been so frightened." She passed ineffectual fingers through her hair to straighten it. "And I've ruined my best dress."

By now there was a circle of people around them, mouthing inarticulate demands to know what had happened. "I'll phone the police," one man said.

"Leave them alone, leave them alone." A large middle-aged woman, her hair done up in plaits, pushed her comfortable bulk through the ring of spectators. "And don't you phone the police, Mr. Wilkins. They can do that themselves from our house." She put the arm of her woolly dressing gown around Angela's shoulders. "You both come in with me, dear, and I'll fix you a cup of tea while you wash your faces. And then you can get in touch with the police. No sense in having them pushing and pulling and asking questions until you have a cup of tea. Come along." She led Angela toward the door of the house before which they had so nearly been killed. Meekly Mike followed, thankful for the authority of her homely Warwickshire voice.

Half an hour later they sat before the electric fire of Mrs. Goudge's little sitting room. Mike drained the last of his tea and made a secret grimace at Angela. He hated sugar in tea, but Mrs. Goudge had been adamant about putting in four teaspoonfuls. "It'll help you get over the shock." Perhaps she had been right; he was still sore all over, but otherwise he felt none the worse.

Angela was drowned in the dressing gown in which their hostess had first appeared. Mrs. Goudge had insisted on putting on a dress, so that she could give her own capacious garment to Angela, in turn taking the torn dress. Now she was busy sewing up the last of it. "It will be ready in a minute. Won't you have another cup of tea? It would do you good." Both Angela and Mike declined. "If you won't, I'll go and wake Mr. Goudge now. He can sleep through anything. He can take out the motorcar and drive you to the police station. Sometimes I think he'll sleep through the Last Trump." On the whole she looked smug about his singular ability.

"No, no, please." Angela was insistent. "That's very kind, but there's no need. If we might use your telephone to ring up for a taxi, we'll do that. Don't bother your husband."

"I don't suppose you could get a taxi at this time of night. And it would do Mr. Goudge no harm. We've had a motorcar only a year now, and he likes to practice when there isn't too much traffic around." She looked up reassuringly. "But don't worry. He's a very good driver."

"Oh, please. I really mean it. Just let me try to get a taxi first. May I use the telephone? I'm sure Mr. Goudge is a splendid driver, but we'd really prefer to take a taxi."

Looking a bit nonplused at having the good services of her husband refused, Mrs. Goudge indicated the telephone in the entrance hall. "And this is all ready for you to put on as soon as you like. Perhaps it's not a first-rate job, but it will look perfectly good at night."

Angela came back. "The taxi will be here in five minutes. If I could just slip my dress on now?" Mrs. Goudge vanished into the kitchen with her. In a minute or two they returned. Angela's dress looked neat, her face was washed and her hair combed. Through the knees of the baggy stockings that Mrs. Goudge had lent her, Mike could see the plaster covering the cuts on her legs, but otherwise she was thoroughly presentable.

They had already thanked Mrs. Goudge wholeheartedly when the taxi arrived. As they said goodbye, she grudgingly admitted that Mr. Goudge would no doubt be thankful for having his slumbers undisturbed.

Angela turned to wave through the rear window. "The police station, please," Mike said to the driver.

Like a flash Angela turned around and faced forward. Her nails dug into Mike's arm. "No, darling, let's go and get the car first. We can drive to the police station." Although her voice had been unusually loud as she spoke, she increased its volume as she leaned toward the back of the driver's head. "Just take us to the car park, driver, please. My husband and I can drive from there." She gave him directions, then leaned back.

Mike started to speak, but she reached up and put her hand over his mouth. He remained silent until they were deposited at the entrance to the car park.

Angela had unlocked the car and was already starting the motor by the time he came from paying off the taxi. "Well, what was that about?" he asked as he climbed in.

She ground away at the starter. "This damned battery is getting feeble. I'll have to have it replaced." The engine turned over. "Thank heaven. I'd hate to try to get a mechanic at this time of the night. We couldn't go to the police, could we? At least, you couldn't."

"Why not?"

"They might check up on your entry, and the authorities don't take very kindly, I should imagine, to aliens who are in the country without a proper permit."

He forced himself to take a breath before answering. "What do you mean?"

"Oh, Mike, can't we drop the masquerade? It's bad enough to be nearly mad worrying about Jim without having to worry about you, too. I don't imagine that you can be in the country legally or you wouldn't be calling yourself Michael Edwards. And certainly you wouldn't be pretending to be the son of that nice Mrs. Edwards. I've never seen two people more unlike." She reached forward to push in the choke. "At least it seems that way to me. But perhaps that's only because I knew you the moment we met."

He felt as if he had been hit a second time. Not in the shoulder but hard in the belly. She was so sure that there was little point in trying to convince her otherwise. "All right," he said slowly. "How did you know?"

"My dear Mike, do you suppose for a moment that anyone like Jim, loving someone as he loves you, could fail to show his brother's picture to his girl?" He stared at her, but she kept her eyes on the road ahead of them. "You're not a very good cloak-and-dagger man, you know. When you asked me if there were a lot of men in my life, you would have made me suspicious of you if I hadn't already known who you were. Obviously Dame Millicent would have told you about Jim before I arrived at the party last night. Even if you were Mrs. Edwards's son, she would have had to tell you both, to stop you from making a tactless remark to me. And, since I knew that you had heard of Jim, your asking about him would have meant either that you were a remarkably maladroit person or that you wanted to find out more about him." She turned briefly toward him and smiled wanly. "So I might have guessed about you even if I hadn't seen the picture."

CHAPTER EIGHT

UNAWARE OF how much she reminded Angela and Mike of Mrs. Goudge, Dame Millicent hitched her sensible long dressing gown around her to make it airtight. Her slippered feet rested comfortably on the slowly heaving flank of Iseult, who had taken up her sleeping position as near as possible to the fire. But it was a coal fire, stirred into renewed life, not an electric bar of glowing red, as Mrs. Goudge's had been, and the idea of offering tea had never entered Dame Millicent's head.

"Michael, would you be so kind as to give me a little more whiskey while you refresh Angela's glass?" she sighed deeply. "I do sympathize with you, but I must say I should love to have been there. A pity you didn't have a pistol. You might have shot at their tires."

"Yes, I suppose I might have," Mike said, "if only I knew how to shoot one. You don't by any chance carry a pistol yourself, do you?"

"Good heavens, no. I shouldn't dream of such a thing. But it would have been most convenient in one of my books. Thank goodness that I have had a good deal of vicarious experience of crime, for I have no doubt that it will be useful to us. What we must do now is to make a plan."

Mike looked discouraged. "I do appreciate everything that you've done, but I think you'd better back out of this. I haven't even got a workable plan for myself. I had hoped that if I could get to know Angela I might find out something about Jim's disappearance. And I thought there might be a chance of stumbling on something if I could get into Doddington Hall. But it would be blind luck if I did.

"What's more important, however, is that if those men in the car were really trying to run us down, it means putting all of you in danger if I stay around. I think the best thing I can do is to hand myself in to the Immigration authorities, tell them why I came into the country, and hope that they'll simply turn me over to the Embassy to put on a flight home. I doubt that they would be very severe if I turned myself in."

"Mike." Angela was almost inaudible. "You're not forgetting Jim, are you? You know and I know that he didn't desert to the Russians, and we've got to prove it. We owe him that, don't we?"

"I'm not forgetting Jim. Believe me, I'm not. But I don't think that we are particularly well equipped to find out what happened. If I were to turn myself in, perhaps that would make the authorities believe that I was serious in being sure that Jim hadn't willingly gone over to the Russians. And perhaps that would make them work harder at finding out what really happened." His face reflected the awareness that he wasn't very convincing.

"Don't be an ass," Angela said shortly, reminding Mike of her manner toward the interfering man in briefs. "They've been at this thing constantly ever since Jim disappeared. I've talked to half a dozen different men from the government already. The only thing is, I'm sure they are convinced he has defected of his own free will. Giving yourself up wouldn't make any difference at all to that."

"I don't trust them all the same." Dame Millicent looked severe. "I know that our English, even British, Intelligence is the best in the world, but there is nothing to equal the ability of a private person with a good brain, unfettered by routine and channels. I believe that I proved that fairly conclusively in *The Curse of Carnigham Court*, didn't I, Florence?"

Mrs. Edwards drew the comforter more tightly around her feet, thanking her lucky stars that she had had the wit to bring it with her when Millicent awakened her. "Of course you did," she said loyally. "I thought it was a wonderful book." She turned to Mike. "And don't talk about giving yourself up. I haven't any intention of letting you spoil my holiday, quite aside from the fact that you might not like going to prison."

"Don't forget that you might go too, if I got caught, Mrs. Edwards. After all, you have been passing me off as your son, and that would surely make you an accessory."

"Nonsense. I thought that all out while you were still sick. I'm sure it isn't a crime to say that you're my son. After all, I didn't get you into the country, and I haven't lied. Not to the police, at least. If we were all locked up for lies that we tell at cocktail parties, there wouldn't be a free man in either England or America. And as for its being physically dangerous for us, that doesn't make any sense either. If that car tonight had anything to do with your brother's disappearance, and if they were trying to get rid of you, they would already know that you're not my son, and they would probably know that Millicent and Angela know it too. And that Per—that Mr. Hetherege—must know it. If it makes any difference to them that we all know it, your going to the authorities wouldn't make us any safer. We would still be in danger."

"I'm sorry" was the best that Mike could manage.

"Don't be ridiculous. I love it. It's the first time it's ever happened to me in my life. Aside from the cooking in Blandinsville, I've never been in danger before. I'm sixty years old, and if something happened to me, it wouldn't matter. If it doesn't, I'll at least be out of my rut. And I think I can say that Millicent is enjoying herself, too. So forget about us. Angela is a different matter. I think she ought to go back to London tomorrow, instead of waiting for Monday."

"I've got more reason to worry than any of you. I'm engaged to him." Angela's voice was deliberately flat. "So let's hear no more about turning yourself in, Mike."

"Suits me, but there isn't much way to thank you all. Now what?"

Dame Millicent laid down the paper on which she had been making notes. "We'd better get some things straight before going on. First of all, why do you feel so sure that the car was deliberately trying to hit you and Angela?"

"The lights prove that. They were turned up when the car got close, so that I would be blinded. And the fact that they didn't stop after nearly killing us."

"Possibly, possibly. But I think that if I suddenly saw that I was bearing down on someone I'd turn on the lights out of natural instinct."

"True, but don't forget that they were almost certainly the men we had seen twice before that day. First at the church, then when we were having a drink before dinner. I'm almost positive that the taller of them was the driver of the car. It was certainly the same kind of car, and it was very muddy." Mike shook his head. "I don't think I'm getting hysterical about this, and I'm positive as can be that it wasn't someone else."

"I didn't see their faces," Angela contributed, "but it was a muddy Vauxhall, all right."

"Sounds conclusive to me," said Florence Edwards, then looked embarrassed as she turned to Dame Millicent. "Not that I have your professional experience, but I'm sure Mike is right."

Dame Millicent inclined her head with judicial solemnity. "Right. Then we can take it as established that someone knows who you are and was trying to kill you. Agreed?"

Mike gulped. "Agreed, but I don't feel as calm about all this as you seem. I don't like the idea of making my debut as a corpse."

"Not at all. But there's no sense in getting into a flap about it." Her mouth moved, then was still. "That's one thing we English know. Keep calm in emergencies." Mike wondered for a wild moment whether she had been stiffening her upper lip. "And, if someone knows about you, we can only assume that your presence here is potentially dangerous to them. Probably they are afraid that you either know or will discover something that our own security people have been unable to turn up. And we have to find out what that is."

"How?"

Dame Millicent turned as majestically as her dressing gown would allow. "Don't ask the difficult questions first, Florence. Let's work on what we know, then we may be able to make some progress."

"It sounds to me as if it must be someone connected with Market Doddington." Angela let a hopeless little sigh escape. "It always seems to come back to that place. I'm positive that if it were something else I'd have some idea about it. I think Jim and I knew as much about each other and about each other's activities as any two people possibly could."

"It certainly has something to do with Market Doddington." From an inner pocket Mike hauled out the letter that had first started him on his trip. He read it aloud, then asked Angela, "He talked to you about this, according to the letter. Do you know any more than he says?"

"Not really. Not much, that is."

"Do you have any idea what the project was? I know that he wouldn't talk about it, but he might have given you some hints about why it would change the airplane and the petroleum industries."

Angela took a lock of hair into her mouth and bit it abstractedly.

"He did give me an idea about it once, but I don't know whether I should repeat it. It only came out accidentally, and he made me promise to forget what he said. But I didn't, naturally. Oh, damn, I don't know what to do. But I guess we're all in this together. All right. I took it from what he said that it was some kind of additive that would make petrol about four times as efficient as it is now. I can see why it would change the petroleum industry, but I don't know what he meant about airplanes."

"Whew," Mike said softly. "Well, for one thing, it would mean that the fuel load would have to be only a quarter as large. Which would mean that planes could carry a much larger cargo and many more passengers. But what would be more important is that their flight range could be quadrupled. And that would mean a lot to the military potential of a country. This isn't just a big development; it's fantastic. And any country in the world would give its arm to get it first. A man who could turn it over to a foreign power could write his own ticket with them." Angela had turned pink and looked as if she were about to explode. "Don't erupt. I obviously didn't mean Jim."

"I have never," said Dame Millicent, "understood what took place beneath the bonnet of the mildest-mannered motorcar, let alone in a jet airship. Nonetheless, I can see that it would be important. Worth defecting for. Or—or even murdering for." The word was out. "I'm afraid that we have to face the fact that your brother may not be alive."

"Yes, I know," Mike said somberly, "but I think it's more probable that he has been kidnaped and sent out of the country. Or even blackmailed somehow into going. The awful thing is that one alternative is almost as bad as the other. I hardly know which I'd prefer for him if I had the choice."

"I know," said Angela. "If he's alive, there's always a chance that he will get back."

Florence Edwards interposed with a firmness Mike had not heard before. "I know how painful it is for you both, but let's stop thinking of the worst. If you are going to do anything to find out what happened to your brother, this won't help."

"Right," Dame Millicent looked at her list again. "Now, about the boat that pursued you in the Channel. I suppose it *could* have been some innocent smugglers or something of the sort, but I'm sure it wasn't the Coast Guards. They would have identified themselves."

"They couldn't have been smugglers," said Florence Edwards. "Whatever else, they wouldn't want to call attention to themselves. I think they might have been Frenchmen who thought that the owner of your boat was smuggling valuable cargo into England. Watches or brandy or cigarettes or whatever is most worth hijacking these days."

"Narcotics," Dame Millicent said firmly.

"Yes, I suppose they would be worth smuggling. If nothing else had happened to Mike, I think that would make sense. But it would be too much of a coincidence if a totally different group of people tried to kill him in Stratford. It seems to me that we must assume the two things were connected. They tried to get him on the boat, and when they failed, they followed him here."

"But why would they think of Stratford out of all the places in England he might be going?" Angela frowned. "Obviously, he wasn't going to be a regular American tourist if he were coming ashore illegally."

"Market Doddington, of course, is where he would be headed. All they had to do was to keep an eye out for a recently arrived American in the neighborhood. Unless this part of the world is very different from Blandinsville, it wouldn't take long for the news of a new arrival to get around. And I think it means that there's a large organization at work if he was followed from France and the attempt on his life was made in Stratford."

"It's not much consolation for Mike to know that, but it must be true," said Angela. "All the same, I think it does prove to you and Dame Millicent that there is more to Jim's innocence than just Mike's word and mine. If he had gone to Russia of his own volition, there wouldn't be anything here to cover up, and they wouldn't be worried about Mike's being here."

"If I were in their place," Mike said, "I think I'd simply write a letter to the police and say that there was an American in Lower Doddington who had entered the country illegally. That would seem like a much simpler way of getting me out of their hair than trying to run me down."

"Oh, no!" Mrs. Edwards jerked upright in her chair. "Excuse me, but I don't think so. First of all, they wouldn't want to draw attention to themselves. And, even if they sent an anonymous letter, it would probably make the police wonder why they were afraid to give their names. Oh, no, it wouldn't be a good idea at all. From their point of view, I mean. Much better for them not to let the authorities know at all. This way you won't be able to go to the police for protection, or even to report that an attempt has been made on your life." Suddenly, as if aware for the first time that she had taken over the conversation, she turned pink and leaned back again. "That's the way it seems to me, at least."

"Don't be modest, Florence." Dame Millicent nodded approvingly. "You are doing very well. Very well, indeed." Iseult gave a sleepy groan and rolled over onto her back, her feet waving limply in the air before they slowly subsided. "Oh, do lie still, you beast."

"Thank you." Mrs. Edwards beamed. "I know it's terrible for Angela and Mike, but I must admit that I'm enjoying this. It's like a crossword puzzle. But I have been wondering about your Mr. Plymson. I wonder what he could have to do with your brother's disappearance. He seemed like a nice man in his way, but—well, I ought to confess that, when I was talking to him just before he left the party, I think I said something about Angela's taking Mike to Stratford tonight. I know I shouldn't have, but it slipped out without my thinking. I didn't think it would do any harm. I'm terribly sorry if it did, Mike."

"Jim's letter didn't sound as if he thought Plymson could be involved. He even said that he thought he was too easygoing. So don't worry."

"I should think," said Angela, "that if he wanted Jim not to know that anything was going on at the lab, a pose of being easygoing would be a very good coverup."

"Absolutely," said Dame Millicent. "I never have liked that man. There's nothing I'd put past him. I saw him drop a cigarette stub into a vase of flowers last night. And he wears a blazer with his college crest on it. With," she added virulently, "pen and pencil clipped into the outside pocket. *Capable de tout!*"

"But," said Angela, "even if he is a little hairy-heeled, he *is* the director of Market Doddington, and I think that counts for a lot. Certainly he would never have been put into such an important position unless the authorities had made a thorough investigation of his background."

"Background," snorted Dame Millicent. "He hasn't got any!"

Angela glanced at her watch. "It's two-thirty. I absolutely must go. As it is, my parents will probably think I've either been killed in a car smash or suffered a fate worse than death. I wish I were going to be here on Monday to talk to you all after you've been at Market Doddington. Good luck."

Mike walked out to the car with her, and the two older women straightened the room before going to bed again. "Wake up, Iseult," Dame Millicent said as she emptied her ash tray into the last of the fire. "Time for bed." She bent over to pat the dog's belly. "Good heavens, Florence. As if we hadn't got enough to cope with already. I do believe this damned animal has come into season."

CHAPTER NINE

IT IS LIMEWOOD, ISN'T IT? Or could it be lancewood? I don't think I've ever seen any of his work in lancewood. It's quite rare." Florence brushed the miraculously carved festoon of fruit with a knowing forefinger.

"I'm afraid I don't know." The young man turned pink. "I'm sure I ought to know, but I had never thought to ask. I had always supposed that it was oak. Couldn't it be?"

"Oak doesn't give that kind of crispness. It's much stiffer. None of that wonderful plasticity. I'm afraid it's not lancewood, and you can tell by the striation of the grain that it isn't oak. Gibbons did use oak occasionally, but usually limewood. Occasionally pearwood, even box. But this definitely isn't oak."

Mike listened to Florence in admiration. He was sure that she had not had more than an hour after breakfast that morning to read the book that Dame Millicent had given to her. Whether she would take in Plymson when he arrived was more problematical, but she already had young Mr. Applethwaite atwitch with embarrassment at his own ignorance.

From comfortable chairs at the other end of the long room the Hethereges, brother and sister, sat watching Florence and Mike as they inspected Gibbons's carvings with Plymson's assistant. "Funny damned thing. Told me the other day his name was Plymson. Now he calls himself Applethwaite. Don't like it at all."

"Don't be ridiculous, Peregrine. I introduced him to you myself, and I told you he was called Applethwaite." Dame Millicent screwed up her face at the smell of his pipe. "I don't see how a young man like you can be so forgetful. Sometimes I think you don't try."

"At least I haven't forgotten that he poured himself out a glass of sherry. Looks like a gentleman, too. Don't understand it."

"These fish are a lot like the ones at Belton." Florence smiled soothingly at Mr. Applethwaite. "Perhaps you haven't had a chance to see Belton. I'm sure you would like it."

"The fact is I'm a scientist, and I've never had much time to learn about these things. Mr. Plymson would know about them. He should be—there he is now." Only good manners appeared to be keeping him from breaking and running, once his superior had appeared. But public-school training will tell, and he restrained himself to a barely audible sigh of relief.

"So sorry to be late," Plymson was repeating as he came down the room greeting his guests. If he was dismayed at the presence of Dame Millicent and her brother, he succeeded in hiding the fact. "The meeting went on a good bit longer than I had expected. But I hope you've had a chance to look at the Gibbons work here."

"Mr. Applethwaite has been most helpful," Florence said maliciously. "What a lovely room it is. The overmantel is one of the best things I've ever seen. It certainly is as good as the Modena panel, don't you think?"

"Wish I could say, but I've never had a chance to see it. Still, I do think this room bears comparison with his work at Chatsworth and Blenheim."

"In this piece thou hast thyself outdone," Florence murmured.

"Beg your pardon?"

"Sorry. I was only repeating what Nahum Tate said about Gibbons. But it does apply here. You were quite right about how good this room is. I envy you being able to work here every day."

"I'm afraid one finally ceases to notice it. Even the Hethereges don't seem much interested."

"I believe they used to come here frequently when Lord Doddington owned the house. They know it well."

Their conversational gavotte continued its pretty measures, bows and curtsies interspersed with little cries of "Gadrooned cornices," "Swags and putti." Mike found his attention veering away from Mrs. Edwards's improbable skill to more elemental matters. When he was able to interject momentarily, he asked Plymson, "Is there a bathroom near here?"

"The lavatory," Plymson corrected him, "is out of the end door and down the corridor to the left." He swung back to Florence without missing the beat.

"I don't see why we had to come," Peregrine grumbled. "I should have stayed at home to see that Collins cleared away the weeds by the hives. If they get any higher, the bees won't be able to get back into the hives. Besides," he added "we won't find out a damned thing by sitting here. That fellow's ruined the room anyway. It was a fool's errand."

Once he had closed the door into the hall, Mike found himself in another world. As he had thought before when visiting English country houses, it was like going behind the scenery to enter the servants' quarters. There had probably been a baize door behind the carved one. Crystal, gilt, and Gibbons gave way to the severely practical. Coronado had put down hair carpet runners and painted the walls corporation cream, but the change in atmosphere was unmistakable. Probably the real running of Doddington went on here now, just as the easy life of the house had once been maintained by servants who never visited the state rooms he had just quitted.

Uncertainly, he turned to the left, as he had been directed. For a moment he thought of the possibility of neglecting his real errand and looking around the house, but he immediately dismissed the idea. He wouldn't even know where to look. Probably Mr. Hetherege had been right in complaining all during the drive about the impracticability of the trip. Besides, there was no possible way he could pretend to mistake his way in order to get into the severely modern buildings that lay behind the house. Applethwaite had said that they contained the laboratories, and that the house was given over to offices.

As he walked down the corridor, he passed two doorways with new flush doors installed in them, bearing name plates. Perhaps Jim had occupied one of the rooms behind them. It didn't take big corporations long to make changes like that.

At the end of the corridor a door with ribbed translucent glass proclaimed his destination. As he looked, it opened and a man came out, turning down another corridor without noticing Mike's approach.

"Florence isn't doing badly, is she?" Dame Millicent made an ineffectual pass at subduing her hair. "Personally, I should like a cup of coffee, so I hope she runs out of information soon. I hope they supply some chocolate biscuits. It would be like the Plymson creature to offer us nothing with the coffee. I'd never have guessed she could carry it off so well."

"She ought to know something about it. I primed her last night after dinner."

"You?" Dame Millicent looked hard at him. "Do you know anything about Gibbons?"

"I'm not so stupid as you think, Millie," he said darkly. "I'd rather have ginger nuts than chocolate biscuits. I hope he's got some. That Applethwaite man took himself off pretty quickly once his boss got here. Probably out eating up all the ginger nuts."

"I can't say that I blame him. He probably felt like a mouse. Florence was all but lashing her tail back and forth while she played with him."

Her brother took hold of the arms of his chair and shifted his weight, a sure sign, she knew, that he was annoyed. "Nonsense. You sound like a jealous female, Millie. She just knew a good bit more than he did. She couldn't help it if he was uneducated. She was remarkably quick at picking up what I told her."

But Dame Millicent was not listening. "Peregrine!"

"What's the matter now?"

"Look at Mike."

"Don't be rude, Millie. No use staring at a man just because he had to go to the loo."

"Don't be an ass. Look at him. He's white as a sheet. I wonder what happened."

After coffee with chocolate biscuits, which Peregrine refused to touch, Plymson showed them two or three other rooms and then walked out with them to Dame Millicent's car. He stood on the steps waving as she piloted an unsteady course down the gravel drive between the antiseptically clipped lawns.

"That's where he lives. There beyond the wall." Dame Millicent gestured expansively to a pretty little Queen Anne house set in its own garden past the lodge gates. "It used to be the dower house. I hate to think of his living in it. Molly Doddington would turn over in her grave if she knew." Before she turned her attention back to her steering, she had driven the near wheels over a few feet of lawn, then she headed back in the general direction of the drive.

"Millie, there are times I wish you had never gone out to the States and learned to drive. I don't see how you ever passed your test. Or do they have driving tests out there?"

"Good heavens, look at those nasty brutes." Dame Millicent grimaced. In a long run next to the gatehouse, six enormous male Doberman pinschers threw themselves, snarling, at the high steel fence that enclosed them. She slowed down the car and handed back a pass to the uniformed man who came out of the lodge door. "What are those dogs for?"

The man looked over his shoulder at the pen. "Guard dogs. They're turned loose in the park at night after the lab is closed. Ugly, aren't they? I'd hate to have them after me. Good thing there's a strong fence." He touched his cap in a civilian version of salute and went back to the television set.

They rode in silence, except for the clashing of gears, until they were a few hundred yards down the main road. "Well, Templeman, what happened to you that made you look so white?"

"For heaven's sake, Peregrine, can't you remember to call him Michael? Or Edwards, if you must. Otherwise you're sure to call him Templeman in front of someone else."

"Sorry, Edwards. Michael. What happened?"

Mike frowned. "Not much. But I saw Stevenson coming out of the lavatory." Florence Edwards turned a puzzled face from the front seat. "He was a man who called himself Stevenson. He sat next to me on the plane coming across the ocean. He said he was a manufacturer and that he lived in Liverpool. Then

I thought I saw him again in France the night before I came across the Channel."

*   *   *

Angela turned from the stove. "No, I don't think I've ever met anyone like that. And certainly not with the name of Stevenson. I couldn't pretend that I remember everyone at the Centre, but I imagine that I've met most of them with Jim. There aren't more than about fifty people there. Adults, I mean. There are a few lab boys and secretaries that I don't suppose he ever introduced me to." She resumed pushing the chopped onions, celery, and long, thin strips of red pepper around the frying pan. Then she squeezed two cloves of garlic through a press into the pan.

"I'm not sure I can wait until that's cooked. It smells wonderful."

"Wait you will, all the same. Sorry I'm a bit slow with the supper. Open the wine, would you please? I hope you don't mind a claret with jambalaya, but I think it needs a wine that will fight back."

While Mike was busy with the corkscrew, she spoke again over her shoulder. "Have you see the *Express* today?"

"No. Why?"

"I thought you hadn't. There was an article about Jim."

Carefully he removed the cork before he spoke. "What did it say?"

"A couple from Frinton said they saw him in Moscow. On the street. They said he looked well."

"Were they sure?"

"They said they were."

"I suppose we ought to be thankful he's well." There didn't seem to be much more to say on the subject, and Angela clearly didn't want to talk about it. When he had carried the bottle to the table, he said, "This is a curious place for a girl to live by herself. Four empty floors below you at night. Don't you ever get lonely?"

"Not often. They don't shut off the machines until six, and there are cleaning people about until eight. I don't mind after that. Where else could I possibly find a flat as large as this right in the heart of London at a price I could afford? Not everyone wants to live over a bedding factory." She stirred a large cup of rice into the pan, swirling it around until it glistened with the bacon fat in which the vegetables had been simmering. "The weekends are wonderfully quiet here. Great Marlborough Street is almost empty on Sundays."

When he had got out of the taxi from Paddington, Mike had telephoned from a corner call box, and she had dropped the front-door key out of a window, so that he could get into the building. "There weren't many people around when I came in."

She frowned. "If you hadn't been so insistent, I think I'd have asked you not to come. Several government officials have talked to me at work, and though they have never been here, I have wondered whether they might be keeping an eye on this flat." She turned off the heat and carried the pan to the table. "It wouldn't do for them to see you here."

"Don't worry. Since they don't even know I'm in the country, they're not apt to be looking for me." He watched as she stirred the mixture of golden rice and vegetables into the casserole that already contained large pink prawns, chunks of ham, and tiny slices of hot Spanish sausage. "Where did you learn to make this?"

"From Jim, of course." She tucked a bay leaf into the side of the container, then sprinkled the other ingredients with peeled tomatoes. "I always think it looks like a Matisse painting." She bent and smelled the casserole. "I'll put in a little water for the rice, and it should be ready to eat in another half hour. How about a drink now? All the same, I do worry about your being seen." She returned the casserole to the cooker.

Mike took the bottle she handed him and poured icy Chambéry into two glasses that scarcely changed color as they filled with the wheat-pale vermouth. "It was probably selfish of me to insist on coming, but I did want to ask you about Stevenson. Even more, I suppose, I just plain wanted to see you. I hate to think of your being alone here all week."

He stopped. If he said more, he would say too much. Already, he was aware, he felt more for Angela than was strictly comfortable, and to give chaotic emotions the form of words was to invest them with more validity than he intended. He was certainly not falling in love with his brother's girl, and he had no intention of letting himself do so. That, as he had told himself before, was not the purpose of this operation. He raised his glass. "Here's to you, and to the success of this operation."

"What's the real purpose of this operation, as you call it, Mike? I wonder whether you've thought it through. I'm afraid you're just getting yourself into trouble, without much chance of ever finding out anything. Even if you did find out something, what could you do about it?" There was discouragement as well as challenge in her voice.

He walked to the window. The lights of Regent Street led in a graceful curve to the brighter glow of Piccadilly Circus. He looked at them as he answered. "I don't know exactly. At the very worst I suppose I have to satisfy myself if I can. Maybe what I feel is only curiosity, but I hope that it's an attempt to do whatever is due to Jim—although if I'm not sure what is due." Even to himself his voice sounded as discouraged as hers had.

"But what could you do?"

He violently threw back the curtain cord he had been twisting. "Damned if I know. But if I could demonstrate that Jim didn't go of his own free will, that would be something. Probably if I could do that, I could go directly to the police or whoever I ought to see. I doubt that they would put me in the jug if I could prove that my being here had a real reason. I felt as if I had made the first step, even if it was a pretty feeble one, when I saw Stevenson today. It made me feel that I wasn't on the wrong track altogether." The cord swung, then snagged in the curtain. "But, whatever else, I can't do nothing. Do you understand?"

When he turned toward Angela, he saw tears forming in her eyes. "Of course I understand, Mike. Sorry I asked." She stood up. "I'd better stir the jambalaya."

Through the kitchen door he could hear her at the stove, and in a moment a gusty aroma came through, making him almost faint with hunger. "Angela?"

"Yes?" came back in the bemused tones of a woman intent on cooking.

"How late did you say they worked here?"

"The cleaning men leave about eight."

"I thought I heard a noise downstairs. They must be working late."

"Not very. It isn't eight-thirty yet, is it?"

In a moment she was back, carrying her glass, which she had emptied in the kitchen. There were no traces of tears now. "It looks good. Let's give it another ten minutes. Could I have more vermouth, please?"

She walked over to the record player and turned a switch, then put a record on the turntable. "Remember this?" In a moment the familiar opening of the *Grosse Fuge* filled the room. She came back and sat down on the sofa beside Mike. They were silent, and Mike wondered whether she was aware of what he had been thinking about her.

"Mr. Templeman."

The voice came from the door behind them. Angela gave a half-born scream and swung around, inadvertently throwing most of the contents of her glass onto Mike. More slowly he turned. In the doorway to the stairs stood the two men they had seen three times before: in the church at Stratford, in front of the Dirty Duck, and last in the muddy Vauxhall that had nearly killed them in Blunt Lane.

"Awkward stairs, miss. You ought to get a light. Somebody might get hurt." The taller man kept his revolver pointed directly at Angela as he spoke. His companion's gun was leveled at Mike. "Just stay where you are." He kicked the door shut behind him without looking at it and came around the end of the sofa.

The other man moved toward the record player. "Is this the best music you've got? It makes me sick."

"Leave it alone, Bert." The tall man's voice was quiet, expressionless. "It doesn't matter whether you like it or not." Without answering, Bert came back and stood in front of Mike. Clearly he was used to being told what to do by his companion.

Sitting back on the deep sofa, Mike knew that he was completely helpless. Even if there were no one to impede him, getting up would be an awkward business. Speed would be impossible. There was nothing to do but stay where he was, whatever the intruders had in mind.

The tall man sniffed. "Ready for your tea, are you? Keep them covered, Bert." He walked casually into the kitchen and lifted the lid of the casserole. "Smells good." He caught up a prawn in his left hand and waved it until it was cool, then put it into his mouth. He turned off the burner. "No use in wasting them." He came back into the sitting room and in one hand picked up a straight chair from the table that Angela had set. With the gun pointed at the sofa again, he put the chair down facing Mike and Angela.

"Get up, Mr. Templeman." He gestured at Mike with the gun. "And don't try anything. Nobody would hear this over the noise of the gramophone."

Mike stood up. For one bad moment he felt his knees wobble as he straightened them, but he got them under control before he thought their tremor could be noticed. His unsteadiness was due to the awkwardness of rising from the sofa, but it might have looked like fear. Whether it was Angela or the two gunmen that he didn't want to see his knees wobble, he couldn't have said. "What do you want?"

"You'll see." The tall man's voice sounded as businesslike as if he were completing a commercial transaction. "Come over here and sit down in this chair. And don't worry about your knees shaking. It happens to the best of us."

Slowly Mike walked to the chair and stood facing it, his back to Angela. "Sit down, I said." The man had still not raised his voice. "Just sit down." Mike turned and sat down stiffly. "Relax. You might as well be comfortable."

When Mike was in the chair, the tall man stepped behind him out of sight. "All right, I've got you both covered. Get the curtain cord, Bert."

As Mike watched, Bert went to the window where he had been standing a few minutes before. He put down his gun on a little table and took out a pocket knife. Without hurry he pulled the curtains closed, opened the blade of the knife, and neatly cut off four feet of cord.

Mike felt the barrel of the gun pressed against the back of

his head. "Now put your hands behind you, Mr. Templeman. You'll be all right if you don't make a nuisance of yourself." Mike was slow to move, and for the first time the other's voice rang with authority. "Behind you. And fast!" Reluctantly he obeyed.

Bert came toward them carrying the cord in one hand, his gun in the other. "All right, Bert." He spoke again with the low, almost agreeable tones he had previously used. "Cross your hands, Mr. Templeman." Bert moved out of Mike's vision, and then he felt the cord being wrapped around his wrists. The cord was tight, although not painfully so, and Mike knew that he would not be able to wriggle his hands apart, either now or later. Then they were forced upward as Bert tied them firmly to the crosspiece in the middle of the chairback.

"Okay, that ought to hold him." Bert gave a final testing tug at the cord and came back into sight. Mike's feet were not tied, but he could not even rise without taking the chair with him. There was nothing he could do now. Both he and Angela were totally at the mercy of the two men.

The tall man took the other chair from the table, turned it around, and sat six feet away, between Angela and Mike, where he could easily cover them both. Bert sat at the other end of the sofa, opposite him in an easy chair. They wore the checked sports coats Mike had seen at Stratford, and in spite of the guns still looked more like touts in a movie than like killers. Even more, Mike found himself thinking incongruously, like members of the chorus in a provincial English production of *Guys and Dolls*.

But any coziness in their appearance was dispelled by the tall man's words. "Now, Mr. Templeman, we want to talk seriously to you. We've had enough of your trying to interfere in what doesn't concern you. Our advice to you is to clear out. The best thing would be for you to get back across the Channel the way you came. But, whatever you do, just keep away from Market Doddington. I can promise you that you're not going to find anything out. We don't much want to kill you, but you might have a nasty accident if you don't agree. Do you understand?"

"You tried hard enough to kill me in Stratford," Mike said

sullenly. It was foolish to talk back, and he knew that he should have kept his mouth shut.

"No. You're mistaken there. I'm a better driver than you think. I could have killed you if I had wanted to. We wanted to frighten you, and I think we did. There's another thing, too. Don't think that you can throw yourself on the mercy of the police, and that you will be forgiven for coming into the country illegally. It might work, but if you tried it, I'm afraid we'd have to come back and visit Miss Woodhouse. A few minutes with a knife or a little acid, and she wouldn't be as pretty as she is now." He glanced at Angela, who had gone totally white. "Or as pretty as she was when we came in. I doubt that it would bother your brother much, but you wouldn't like it."

"You bastard," Mike said softly.

"Of course the police would give her protection for a while, but they have a forgetful way about them. After a month or two, they have other things to do. And then we would pay a visit to Miss Woodhouse again. Understand?"

Mike nodded. From the record player he could hear the quartet beginning the coda.

"That's good." He got up and came over to Mike. With his gun still in his right hand, he put his left on the top of the chair. "Now stand up, Mr. Templeman. I'll help you and hold the chair. I want you to turn around and face that table."

Mike did not move, and the man pushed the chair forward, toppling Mike to his feet. "Stand up." He gave the back of the chair a sharp pull upward, making Mike wince with pain at the strain on his arms. "We're not going to hurt you."

At last Mike turned toward the table, the other taking the weight of the chair off his arms. "Sit down again." Mike obeyed.

The laconic Bert spoke. "It's your turn, miss." Out of the corner of his eye Mike saw him rise lazily and approach her as she sat on the sofa. "Go over to the table."

For the first time since the man had entered, Angela spoke. "No, I won't," she said. "You can't make me."

"I think we can." The tall man left Mike and came up to her. He stood smiling at her for a moment, then his left hand darted out. Angela screamed as he slapped her. He looked contemplatively at her, then hit her as hard as he could on the other cheek. "Go ahead. Shout as much as you like. No one will hear you." He went to the record player and turned up the volume. The quartet worked to a glittering pyramid of sound as the end approached. The sheer volume was appalling, the scream of strings agonizing. But through it came the quiet voice again. "Now go to the table." Angela got up and walked reluctantly to where he pointed.

"Mr. Templeman, you aren't going to like what we do, but I warn you that, if you so much as move, Miss Woodhouse will be badly hurt, and I'll shoot you without saying another word to you. Please get that clearly in mind." He turned to Angela, and as he did so, the last understated measures of the *Grosse Fuge* sounded. There was a click and the turntable came to rest. The sudden silence was nearly as painful as the preceding noise had been. With a thin smile the tall man turned to his companion. "Put it on again, Bert."

"Oh, Christ," Bert said half to himself, but he went to the machine and lifted the tone arm. "Do I have to?"

"Go on, Bert, put it on again." The magnified sound of the needle on the record scratched through the room, then came the majestic opening notes of the first fugue, almost unrecognizable in their volume. "That's right, Bert. Now come back here."

Angela stood hesitantly beside the table. Bert approached her from the rear and put his arms around her, pinioning her arms to her side. In a burst of anger she raised her right foot and brought the heel down hard on his instep. Bert grunted with pain but kept his hold fast on her. "You bitch! This is going to be a pleasure."

The tall man stood in front of Angela, shaking his head from side to side. "You shouldn't have done that." With the same amazing rapidity of movement he slapped her again, his fingers leaving a white pattern on her flushed face. Without bothering to watch her reaction, he turned to Mike. "Now if you are in any doubt about what we would do to Miss Woodhouse, perhaps this will convince you."

He reached for her left hand and took it in a firm grip. "Put her down, Bert." Obediently the other bent forward over Angela, so that she was forced to lean on the table with the elbow of the arm that the tall man held. Slowly, almost gently, he pulled her hand down until the forearm was flat on the table-cloth. Then he turned it over so that the palm hung over the sharp edge of the table.

He took a quick, amused look at Mike before he raised the gun and smashed its butt down on Angela's arm just above the edge of the table. Her scream rose above the Beethoven. Mike had time only to see the jagged edge of bone projecting through the skin before Bert removed his arms and let her slump to the floor. Unperturbed, the fugue, magnified to a point near pain, maintained the detached serenity of its progress.

CHAPTER TEN

Mike slept most of the way to Stratford, waking only for the change at Leamington. He had been awake all night, except for a few fitful naps on a bench at the hospital. Even if there had been a decent place to sleep, he probably would have been unable to take full advantage of it.

In spite of the pain of her arm, Angela had managed to untie the cord around his wrists with her one working hand, and he had supported her down the stairs and got her into a taxi in Regent Street. At the hospital he had walked miserably up and down the waiting room of the emergency unit after she was wheeled away by a male attendant. "It won't be a long operation," he was told, "but don't count on her being out of the operating room for some time. We've got to get ready for it first."

It was nearly midnight before a young surgeon came to speak to him. "It was a nasty break, but there shouldn't be any trouble. She'll have to stay here for two or three days for observation while we keep her pumped full of antibiotics. Perhaps less time if all goes well. After that, she ought to be perfectly all right. She'll have a cast for several weeks, but it won't be too painful. How in heaven's name did she manage to fall so hard? Down the stairs?"

"The stairs to her flat are steep, and there isn't a good light," Mike said truthfully. "It's easy enough to trip on them."

In the morning, after an uncomfortable night on a bench in the waiting room, he had been allowed to see her briefly. "No use your staying here," she said. "Please go back to Dame Millicent's."

"What will you do when you get out of this place?"

"I'll get someone from the office to go with me to help pack, and then I'll come back home myself. Don't worry about me. I'll see you when I get back."

"I'm afraid you won't," said Mike. "I think I'm going to take their advice and leave the country. I'm not getting anywhere in the first place, and in the second, I'll be damned if I'm taking any chances on their doing anything more to you."

"Don't be a fool," she said. "I'm not being brave, but I thought it over while I was having breakfast. You are the only one who is in danger now. What they did to me was only to convince you that you ought to leave, not because they really had anything against me. If you leave now, I can't blame you, because they might do something worse to you. But I'm perfectly safe. I'm in the hospital now, and when I get home, I'll be with the family, so don't consider me when you make your decision. The only people to consider are you and—and Jim."

"I don't think I can take a chance on your being hurt again."

"But how about Jim?" she asked pitilessly, her voice almost hard. "Perhaps we don't know why, but you obviously represent a threat to someone, or they wouldn't be so anxious to get you out of the country. If ever we can do anything for Jim, it looks to me as if it is now." And so they had left it, with Mike's agreeing reluctantly to return to Lower Doddington.

As he came through the barrier and surrendered his ticket, he saw Dame Millicent striding up and down, leaving a little whirl of cigarette ashes as she made the turns. She waved at him with less ebullience than he was used to. He hoped she hadn't minded coming to the station for him.

"Delighted," she answered his tentative apology with what he took for real enthusiasm. "I had to come to Stratford to shop in any case. No trouble at all." But her face fell into unaccustomed solemnity. "Wait until we're in the car and then you can tell me everything that happened."

Sitting in stately solitude on the back seat was Iseult, looking only slightly embarrassed by the pair of pants she wore, reminding Mike of the briefs on the man in Blunt Lane. "No reason to put her into kennel just because she's in season," her mistress explained. "At home she's perfectly safe in the back garden from those brutes of dogs that keep circling the place. And she can wear these in the car. I'm sure she needs a change of scenery occasionally." She let in the clutch and catapulted them forward.

Dame Millicent's nonchalant direction of the car as if it were a wayward horse made him almost wish for the gunmen of the night before in preference to the dangers of being her passenger. But her manner remained subdued in spite of her disregard of their safety. She listened intently as he told her what had happened in Angela's flat, asking only the briefest and most relevant questions, interrupting only to express her sympathy.

"She seems in pretty good shape, considering what she went through," he finished his account. "I feel as if I ought to give it all up, but I don't see how I can, so long as she insists that she is safe. I'm sure now that Plymson or Stevenson, or probably both of them, got worried when they realized that I might have seen Stevenson, and that they had me followed to London. They are obviously working together."

"I doubt if they were," said Dame Millicent. "And certainly they are not now." She looked grave. "Mr. Plymson is dead. His body was found this morning."

Mike stared at her. "What happened?"

"I don't know. All that I can tell you is what the cleaning woman said when she came in today. She lives in Market Doddington, and her husband is a gardener at the Hall. Plymson was killed by those horrible dogs we saw yesterday, and his body was found in the park, near the entrance to the garden of the dower house. The man who is in charge of the dogs found him about seven. His body had been very badly savaged." She sounded the horn furiously at a bicyclist. "I didn't think I should ever feel sorry for him, but I do. I rather wish I had been friendlier. In spite of the blazer."

"But how could it have happened? After all, he was the director of the entire place, and he would have known about the guard dogs."

"Of course he did. And normally when he had to go into the Hall at night, he went to the front gates and was taken in by the man in charge of the dogs. Evidently that's what all the employees did. And they'd ring up the lodge when they wanted to leave. Or that's what Mrs. Clotworthy said, at least. But he apparently walked out the gate of his garden into the slype last night."

"The what?"

"The slype, the passage that leads from his garden into the park. It's about ten yards long and runs between two high stone walls. There are wrought-iron gates at either end of it, one into the garden, one into the park. Molly Doddington used to have a fine herbaceous border along either side of the path, but Plymson had replaced it with begonias. Probably easier to take care of. Just the sort of flower he *would* like." She looked contrite. "Sorry, I shouldn't say that of him now that he's dead, I suppose, but he really was a begonia type.

"Last night he was watering the garden, and he had gone into the slype to tend those unspeakable flowers. I suppose he didn't notice that the gate into the park was open. Or perhaps he had forgotten about the dogs. They're so fast and so silent that they must have been upon him before he knew what was happening. This morning the hose was still running. His body was in a great pool of water. Poor devil." She sighed. "But, if he had left the herbaceous border alone, it would never have happened. I hope that they will at least get rid of those atrocious brutes of dogs."

"Didn't anyone notice that he was missing?"

"He's lived alone ever since his wife died. He had a cook and a daily, but they both go home at night. So there wasn't anyone to notice. Somehow that makes it worse, doesn't it?"

Mike frowned. "Do you think there is a chance that it wasn't an accident?"

"Nonsense. No man would commit suicide in that way; it would be almost the worst way that I could imagine."

"Supposing it wasn't suicide?"

"Murder? What would be the point of that? If Plymson was working for the Russians, their own people wouldn't kill him. It doesn't make sense."

"I suppose it doesn't. But, you know, it would be a good way to kill a man. Get the attention of the dogs, then drop him over the wall. They would be on him at once, and there would be no other marks on him. Even," and he shivered, "if the body was in any condition to be examined. Any scratches or bruises from a struggle would naturally be attributed to what the dogs had done."

"What a bloody mind you have, Michael." She threw him a look of admiration. "But it's not a bad idea at all. You know, that might be useful in a book I'm writing now. Perhaps it would be better to make it a bull." She was lost for a moment in consideration. "But, no, that couldn't have been the way with the Plymson crea—with poor Mr. Plymson. The hose, you see. That's conclusive."

"I don't think so. It could be thrown over the wall. Or even pushed through the opening in a gate. Hoses are fairly rigid, and they could be pushed. If it were not in the right position, anyone would assume that he had dropped it or thrown it when the dogs came."

"Possibly. But the fact remains that there was no reason for him to be murdered. Think it over. You'll find that I'm right."

Mike nodded, keeping his reservations to himself. He could not think of a reasonable objection to what she had said, but he remained unconvinced.

He had tea alone with Dame Millicent and her brother. Angela's parents had invited Mrs. Edwards to come with them for lunch in Stratford and a visit to Ragley Hall. "I'll have to tell them about Angela when they come back," he said. "She thought it would be better that way than if she were to telephone. I'll say she fell down the stairs. I can't tell them what actually happened."

"Her father's a doctor. I don't see why he would get upset about a broken arm." Dame Millicent swept another piece of chocolate cake onto her plate.

"Probably he wouldn't, but she was afraid her mother might worry. Anyway, it's a good thing her father is a doctor. He can keep an eye on her arm when she gets here. She wants to go back to work next Monday, but I hope he can convince her she ought to take more rest. It was a bad break, and she must still be suffering from shock."

Peregrine Hetherege looked up. "May I have another cup, please, Millie? Broken arms don't need to be coddled. Broke mine years ago on a dig in Sicily. Silly young chap let his pick slip and hit me. Medico put me in plaster and I was back at the dig in the afternoon. Hurt like hell, but it didn't do me a bit of harm. Still, I suppose women are different. Break easier and take longer to mend. Good cake, even if it is chocolate."

"Would you and Michael like to take Iseult for a walk after tea? You could go down to the White Hart."

Peregrine wiped a piece of chocolate off his mustache. "Wouldn't mind a pint, but don't ask me to take that bitch with us. Every dog in the village would be after her. Have to beat them off with my stick. Put on those damned silly pants and take her for a drive if she needs an outing. Why do you want us to go to the White Hart, eh? Think we'll find out something there? Not a bad idea. But, mind you, no bitch."

The disconsolate Iseult watched Mike and Peregrine from a front window as they set out for the pub. Outside the garden gate a trio of would-be Tristrams marched up and down, growling as they passed each other, pausing occasionally to give amorous sniffs in the direction of the house. "Put your money on the lop-eared mongrel," Peregrine advised Mike as he aimed a swipe of his stick at a shivering whippet. "They always get there ahead of the pure-bred dogs. Damned nuisance that Millie insists on keeping her at home."

Despite its name and Tudor exterior, there was nothing Olde

English about the White Hart. Two of the walls of the public
bar were almost covered with dusty glass cases containing
stuffed fish with labels giving their weight and the date on
which they were caught. Screwed to the floor along another
wall stood a row of red plush tip-up seats, apparently salvaged
from some cinema long since defunct. A sound country pub
with no nonsense, as Peregrine had said.

Mike's watch stood at just after six, and they were the first
customers. "Evening, Watkins," said Peregrine and leaned on the
bar. Mike followed suit.

"Evening, Mr. Hetherege." The pub keeper removed a cloth
of dubious cleanliness from the beer handles. "Fine day." He
switched on a row of lights behind him, squinted without interest at the cloth, and gave the bar a desultory wipe. He was
a heavy man of about Peregrine's age, with a bald, sweaty head.
"Too hot, though."

"Mmm." Peregrine pulled at his pipe as if he had forgotten
why he was in the pub. Watkins passed the cloth over the bar
again, making Peregrine lift his elbow. Silence hung heavy, and
Mike felt that he was the only one who would consider breaking it.

"Like something?" Watkins asked despondently, as if afraid
the answer would be affirmative.

"Two pints of bitter, please." Peregrine waited until the drink
was slid along the bar, gave one to Mike, and said, "Mr. Edwards. Friend of my sister's. American." He took a long swallow
of his beer and resumed looking down at the bar, apparently
wearied by the length of what he had said.

"Evening, sir." That seemed to exhaust Watkins' conversational repertoire, and he puckered his lips in a silent whistle,
looking out the window. There was no noise except the dripping
of the beer tap. Watkins gave it a bash, and it was silent.

Mike applied himself to the beer. It had been a mistake to
come with Peregrine, who obviously didn't even know how to get
a pub keeper into conversation. Dame Millicent would have
been a whiz at it, although he had to admit that he could not
imagine that formidable lady in this pub. He stole a reproachful

glance at Peregrine, who, to his surprise, looked back and gave him a merry smile and a long wink from under the shelter of the brim of his floppy tweed hat.

"Need a puppy, Watkins?"

"No, sir, can't say I do."

"Sister's bitch is on heat. Will you have a drink with us?"

"Thank you, sir, that's very kind." He filled a glass and held it up before he drank. "Your good health."

"She'll probably have a litter. She's careless." Peregrine raised his glass to the publican. "My sister, I mean."

"That's the way with bitches." Watkins nodded in sad agreement. "The dog, I mean." Then his face brightened. "Did you hear about Mr. Plymson in Market Doddington?"

Peregrine looked inquiring.

"Dogs ate him."

Peregrine pursed his lips and blew out in chagrin, but he said nothing.

"Six dogs. Not much but bones left, I hear."

"Mmm." How Peregrine managed to get sagacity, inquiry, and subdued sympathy into a single monotone was beyond Mike.

"Went out to water his gloxinias, and they were on him like a flash. Guard dogs for the park. Crump tells me . . ." He stopped to look at Mike. "Crump's the village policeman here. Crump tells me *he* thinks they'll get the dogs destroyed. He says they cost a thousand pounds apiece. Trained killers, they are. Six thousand quid down the drain." He took a long swallow of beer with relish. "Crump says it's a clear case of Death by Misadventure. That Crump! He can't see past the end of his nose. But I'll wager the coroner isn't any better." He paused and looked up and down the bar as if suspecting that someone had come silently in to hear his conclusion. "There's something funny about it all. Ever since that Yank—begging your pardon, sir—disappeared, I wouldn't trust anything that happened at the Hall."

Peregrine nodded sagely, his pipe waggling in his mouth.

"We used to see a lot of Yanks in here in years past when the Americans were in Nether Otford," Watkins said to Mike in implicit apology. "Most of them were fine chaps, too. Nothing against Yanks myself, whatever the others say." He returned to

Peregrine and the main topic. "The missis and I drove past the Hall this afternoon." He nodded triumphantly. "Nothing. No one. There ought to be a cordon around the place, but there wasn't a soul. That's what I mean," he finished gloomily. "Something funny. I shouldn't be surprised if they're hushing it up."

"Crump been there?"

"Yes, sir. Of course he's got no more business there than I have, but he went up this afternoon. He said Stubbs . . ." Once more he interrupted himself to look at Mike. "Stubbs is the policeman in Market Doddington. He said Stubbs told him there was a man there who came down from the Home Office, but he went back to London after an hour or two. You see? I reckon that they wouldn't have sent a man down if there wasn't something funny going on. But he went right away, so that they could cover the whole thing up. See what I mean?"

As gloomily as Watkins himself, Peregrine nodded, but such an obvious invitation for more revelations was not going to catch Watkins. "Not that I'd want anyone to know that I had said it, sir."

"Of course not." Peregrine looked shocked at the mere suggestion. Watkins pursed his lips in his noiseless whistle and stared resolutely out of the window. Waiting to be coaxed, Mike thought. Peregrine puffed on silently. At last Watkins walked around the counter with his cloth and waved it ineffectually for a time at the fly-blown cases of fish. "Of course," he said without looking at Mike or Peregrine, "of course, there were the Mysterious Strangers." He darted a glance at Peregrine, who resolutely considered the last of his beer.

"Could we have two more pints, please?"

Watkins returned to his place behind the bar and drew the beer. He returned the glasses to Mike and Peregrine, then turned to straighten the bottles of ginger beer behind him. "The mysterious strangers," he said over his shoulder.

"Mmm," said Peregrine. "Like this beer, Edwards?"

"Very good indeed."

"The mysterious strangers." Watkins looked almost pleading. "Mmm. Yes."

"You've heard about them, sir?"

"No."

"Well," said Watkins, leaning across the beer taps, "I heard about them from my sister-in-law. Silly old bitch, if you'll excuse the expression, sir. But she lives in Market Doddington."

"Next to the baker's shop, doesn't she?"

"No. Just past the Co-op. Ordinarily I wouldn't put much stock in what she tells me, but she said that she has seen Mysterious Strangers going into the Hall gates."

"Why mysterious, Watkins?"

"Well you may ask, sir. Because," and he paused with a sure instinct for dramatic timing that Mike had to admire, "they were wearing masks. Not masks, exactly, but they had handkerchiefs over their faces. Just like the ones in that series *The Con Men* on telly. Do you watch it?"

"Don't think I've seen it."

"I don't get much chance myself, trying to keep the pub open all the time. Bloody licensing hours. But it's exciting. And they wear handkerchiefs to hide their faces."

"Sounds like a good program. When did she see them?"

"Sunday. Sunday afternoon. That's another thing. Why would anyone want to go into the Hall on Sunday? The Centre is closed on Sunday. See what I mean?"

Peregrine shook his head in disbelief. "Sounds very fishy, doesn't it?"

Watkins pursed his lips again, clearly Not Having Told All. Then he played his trump card. "And, what's more, they looked like Russians!"

Fairly transparent handkerchiefs, Mike thought, if she could tell that. But such minor discrepancies had clearly not diminished Watkins's relish. "Silly old bitch, as I was saying, but she couldn't make that up, now could she?"

The discussion of Watkins's sister-in-law's narrative ingenuity was interrupted by the entrance of a man and woman. Obviously strangers, they looked around the pub apprehensively. The woman sniffed at the dusty fish cases. "Can you do sandwiches?" the man asked in a Birmingham accent.

Watkins, caught between the laudable desire to sell his wares and an almost equally strong wish to continue expounding his theories about the Hall, hesitated before he answered. But cupidity triumphed. "Cheese and tomato and chutney. Cheese and tomato. Cheese."

"Henry, I don't like cheese," the woman whined.

"Damned if I am going to drive another hour or two without any food," he answered.

"Oh, all right." She turned to Watkins and changed her tone to one of arch refinement. "Cheese and tomato, please."

Watkins's exposition of the mysteries of Market Doddington was obviously not to be resumed, and when they had finished their beer, Mike and Peregrine left the pub.

Safely out of earshot, Mike said, "My apologies. I thought he wasn't going to say anything, but you had him nearly bursting to talk."

Peregrine repeated the wink that had so surprised Mike earlier. "Caught most of the fish in those cases myself. Can't do that without knowing how to play them. Didn't find out much, though. Watkins is right: Crump is a fool, and Watkins's sister-in-law is a silly bitch. What did you think about the mysterious strangers? How in merry hell could she know that they looked like Russians if they were wearing handkerchiefs?"

"I wonder if she watches *The Con Men* herself. That might explain the handkerchiefs. Was Watkins just telling a good story, or do you think his sister-in-law made up the whole thing?"

"He may have added an artistic touch or two, but I think he was telling what he thought was the truth, on the whole. And I suspect that the woman actually saw something she thought was suspicious. But, God knows, she probably imagined a lot more than she saw. My guess is that she saw somebody going to the Hall on Sunday, and that that's the end of it. No Russians, no handkerchiefs, nothing mysterious. Not that she's necessarily lying, but her imagination helps make a dull existence tolerable. Poor old trout."

CHAPTER ELEVEN

O F COURSE I'll be all right. Don't worry. I'm feeling fine, and I can handle most things perfectly well. Lucky for me that shoes don't have laces nowadays, because I couldn't tie them." Angela smiled. "Except tennis shoes, and I doubt if I'll be playing much tennis while I'm at home."

It was a polite lie, that she felt fine, but not too far from the truth. She was still weak from a day and a half in the hospital, and the arm gave an occasional twitch under the cast, but it was surprisingly free of pain. At least it was true that she could manage perfectly well. All that she had to do was to take a taxi to the station. And the change at Leamington would be nothing.

"I think that's everything." Mary Devlin looked abstractedly around the room. "Except your mac. Can you carry that?"

"Put it in the suitcase if there's room. I think it would be easier to carry it that way than draping it over my bad arm. Even if that would make me look a bit better." Ruefully she held up the cast. "Not very feminine, is it? Least of all this sling."

Mary surveyed her. "I'm not sure. I think it's like wearing great baggy pullovers. The contrast makes you look more fragile than you are." She sighed and put her hands on her opulent hips. "My God, I'd like to look fragile for a change. It would almost be worth breaking my arm if I could manage it. I couldn't get away with a dress like that, and it looks wonderful on you."

"You don't think it's too bright?" Angela asked, obviously not expecting an answer. "I like it too. Salmon pink isn't usually my idea of the color for me, but it seems less garish on a bright day like this." She turned from the table, where she had been writing as she talked. "I can't think of anything else. That's the note for the cleaning woman. . . . I've called the landlord. . . . And, bless you, you've done all the packing. I think I'm ready. Why don't you just go back to the office? I can get a taxi by myself."

"Nonsense," Mary said firmly. "I'll at least carry your suitcase to Oxford Street and wait with you for a taxi." She curled up her nose. "I don't give much of a damn what that old cow Miss Gordon says if I'm late."

The sunny day had brought streams of shoppers, and Angela had to walk behind Mary as they threaded their path along the pavement. In her good forthright Irish way, Mary swung the suitcase, occasionally catching an unwary woman on the knee, but clearing a path for Angela, so that she was in no danger of having her arm banged by passers-by. "Served her right," Mary said over her shoulder after a particularly hard bump had brought a complaining yip from a fat woman whose arms were full of packages. "Sorry," she called in a sweet voice as the woman bent over to retrieve her belongings.

Oxford Street was jammed, and they had trouble making their way to the curb outside Oxford Circus tube station. There were remarkably few taxis about, and those that passed were either occupied by parties of important-looking women in Important Hats, on their way to luncheon parties, or sternly announced by their absence of lights that they were off duty.

Mary looked disconsolately at her watch. She had made a dozen unsuccessful attempts already. "Perhaps it would help if you were to wave your cast and look helpless."

"Don't be so motherly," said Angela. "You're six months younger than I am, and it doesn't become you. Why don't you whiz off? I'll get one on my own."

After many protestations, Mary was persuaded to go back to the office. Angela waved goodbye and turned her attention to taxis. She had less than half an hour to get to Paddington. She and Mary had eaten a bit of the ill-fated jambalaya from the refrigerator, although she had felt that each mouthful might choke her. Lucky she had had something, for she could not remember whether the one-sixteen had a restaurant car. Probably not, nowadays. In any case, there would be a large tea waiting at home, unless she misjudged her mother.

Down the street toward her came a taxi with its light on. She waved at it with her good hand as she shamelessly brandished the cast on her other arm. "Taxi, taxi!" Without bothering to look at her, the driver switched off the light and sailed past. "Beast!" she said aloud and turned to glower malevolently after him. How satisfactory it would be to hear the taxi falter as the engine failed. Or to see it swerve with a blown tire. It would serve him right. For a moment she looked at the stream of pedestrians boiling around the corner from Regent Street, behind the barrier that kept them from venturing into the traffic of Oxford Circus. "Oh, no!" she whispered, then held her breath.

Near the barrier, walking ruthlessly through the tide of shoppers, their eyes fixed upon her, were Bert and his tall companion. Momentarily she was seized by the paralysis of panic, and she stood unable to move, powerless even to remove her eyes from their gaze. She could see them clearly, their faces expressionless, not even intent, only inhuman and pitiless, inexorable. But she knew that they were watching her, and the knowledge that her pink dress made her stand out from the other pedestrians made her feel as if she were trapped in a spotlight.

At last she seized her suitcase, but she remained rooted to the pavement. Unable even to think, she stood watching their slow progress toward her as they bullied their way through the crowd with their checked shoulders, then she skirted the barrier, leapt off the curb into the street, and ran toward them.

The westbound traffic had just been released, and it swept down on her. A horn from behind blasted in her ear, and a large Jaguar swerved to avoid her, but she was powerless now, either to retreat to the safety of the pavement or to climb over the barrier into the crowd. All that was left for her was to continue running around the corner toward Regent Street as fast as she could.

But the barrier was also her protection. Caught behind it, the two men could not get to her. It was much too far for them to go back in the direction they had come. All they could do was to work their way to the end of the barrier around which she had come. And, in the press of the crowd, that would give her a good start.

Out of the corner of her eye she saw them push through the people emerging from the tube station, edging toward the barrier, and as she passed them, the tall man leaned over it to make a grab for her. Without worrying about the squealing brakes behind her, she ran another yard farther out into the street, and his clutching hand fell ineffectually a foot or two from her broken arm.

Ahead of her a policeman in the middle of the road held up his hand to the approaching traffic and blew his whistle. "Miss!" With a burst of speed of which she would have thought herself incapable, she darted past him and raced for the other end of the barrier. "Miss!" The whistle blew again, but it was now blessedly behind her.

It would be useless to try to make her way against the relentless surge of shoppers and office workers. She ignored the end of the barrier when she came level with it, and panted on down the gutter of the street. Mentally she cursed the pink dress that made her so conspicuous, so easy to follow.

Ahead of her was the red beam end of a number 12 bus slowly pulling away from the curb. How could anyone ever have thought it an ugly sight? "Wait, wait!" she screamed with her remaining breath. Her father often said of a plain woman that she had a face like the back end of a London bus. But it was beautiful, beautiful. "Oh, wait," she whispered to herself, but it was already gathering speed, and the West Indian conductor on the rear platform looked disapprovingly at her as she sprinted toward him.

Before the bus could move into the main line of traffic, a car approached fast, sounding its horn. The bus hesitated for its place in the queue, and that was enough for her. With a last lunge she threw her suitcase past the conductor and scrambled aboard.

Impotent to prevent her boarding, the conductor swung himself around and barred the entrance to the lower deck of the bus. "You can't do that. You must get on at the bus stop," he said angrily, but the softness of his speech kept him from sounding forbidding.

Suddenly, without warning, her panting turned into desperate sobs and flooded her cheeks. She sank onto the lower step of the stairs leading to the top deck of the bus as she tried to regain composure. "Miss, don't do that again." He still sounded angry, but he was no longer threatening. He watched her a moment, then said gently, "Are you all right?"

Unable to speak, she nodded her head vehemently. She couldn't imagine what he must think of her or what she must look like, but she didn't really care. At last she managed to say, "Sorry. Yes, I'm all right." She pulled herself to her feet and gathered up her suitcase. "Sorry," she said again before she began climbing the steps.

Near the top she paused. Through the rear window she could see the traffic swinging madly down the curve of Regent Street in disciplined disorder as Oxford Circus receded from her sight. From above the pedestrians looked even more tightly packed on the pavements than they had seemed when she was among them. But nowhere could she see Bert or his tall companion. Not even so much as a checked coat. She looked intently, but for all that she could tell, her wild flight might have been imaginary, a nightmare that had never had tangible reality. A man stood waiting for her to pass, and she moved toward a seat.

Hardly had she sat down when the conductor swung up the stairs. "Where to, miss?" he asked as impersonally as if he had not seen her before.

She looked at him vaguely. Where to? "Where does the bus go?"

Looking out of the window, he had not heard her confused reply. "Where to?" he asked again, more peremptorily this time, and she had to repeat her question.

He looked hard at her, almost as if he saw her for the first time as a person. "Why, to Norwood Junction."

"Where are we going now?"

"To Piccadilly Circus, down the Haymarket, then . . ."

"The Haymarket, please." In her confusion neither of the names made any sense, but the second had a familiar ring.

The conductor took her money, rolled out a ticket, and, as he handed it to her, he asked again in a kind tone, "Sure you're all right, miss?"

She straightened herself. "Quite, thank you," she said coolly. He moved on to the next passenger, then threw her a questioning glance over his shoulder that made her regret her abruptness.

Reality had begun to return as they swept through the maelstrom of Piccadilly Circus, but she could not keep from looking out of the window in futile search of her pursuers. There were no buses in sight behind her, and she knew from experience how improbable it was that they could find a taxi. Following her on foot would be impossible. At the thought of safety she began to feel more composed, even slightly embarrassed at her own disheveled entry onto the bus.

As it slowed down for her stop, Angela carried her suitcase to the top of the stairs. It was a nuisance being one-handed, and she had to lean against the wall as she descended, planting her feet carefully to navigate the steps without mishap, since she could not hang on to the rail. Safely at the bottom, she stood for a moment on the platform until the bus was at a complete standstill.

As she hopped off, she looked up and down the street, knowing she was unnecessarily apprehensive, then headed briskly down Ponton Street toward Leicester Square. Here the crowds were thinner, and she could see no trace of Bert or his companion.

Most of London would be on its way to eat by now. She looked at her watch. It was two minutes past one. Not more than a quarter of an hour had passed since she was waving goodbye to Mary, but it seemed ages. And it was much too late to make the one-sixteen. There was another train just before four, and she could take that. If she were to telephone her parents, they could meet the later train.

It had been a bad week for stockings. She had torn a pair in Stratford, now she had laddered another pair by her wild leap onto the bus. And her inexplicable fit of tears had probably not helped her appearance. She'd better make what repairs she could.

At the crossing to Leicester Square she stood waiting for the traffic to slacken, glad to stand still for a moment. The heel of one of her shoes had loosened in her flight. Perhaps she should change that as well.

The stream of cars thinned out, and she prepared to cross.

She took a tentative step off the curb, then looked down the street again to be sure that she was safe. A blue car approached on her side of the street, then slowed down as if to allow her to cross. Gratefully, she looked up to smile her thanks. Her eyes once more met those of Bert, sitting beside the tall man, who was driving the car.

She was already directly in their path. If the driver accelerated, he would certainly hit her. Reckless of any other cars that might be coming, she instinctively jumped forward. But the car had come to a complete stop, waiting for her to cross, holding up a line of frustrated drivers.

Frightened rather than reassured by the tall man's consideration, she ran forward, her loose heel wobbling. As she reached the curb she looked back over her shoulder. The blue car had drawn up on the opposite side of the street, and Bert was getting out of his door. Once more she stood indecisively, watching as he jumped to the street and the blue car pulled away. Poised like a runner waiting for the gun, his eyes searched the traffic for an opening.

She turned from the street. There lay the peace of Leicester Square, the space behind the fence filled with office workers eating their sandwiches in the sun. Shakespeare looked benignly from his pedestal at the strollers on the wide pavement. But there was no one to whom she could plead for help, no sanctuary in the tranquil scene at the heart of London. And she was too tired to run any more.

Another glance back at Bert. He had found a chink in the traffic and was darting through the cars. Already he was halfway across the street towards her.

Tired or not, she could stand there no longer, accepting the inevitability of a blow, even a stab. Almost hypnotized, she felt that nothing was beyond him, that even the presence of hundreds of spectators would not protect her. She fled down the pavement, and there in front of her lay the sanctuary she had been seeking.

With a whimper of relief she ran down the steps into the women's lavatory. Strange the force of inhibition. While she had not doubted that he would unhesitatingly do her harm in full view of the crowd, she knew that he would never dare to come after her here. And she could stay as long as she wished without fear of intrusion.

She put her suitcase down and stood in the middle of the floor, eyes closed in relief. Then, aware that she was making herself conspicuous, she inserted a penny and entered a cubicle.

When her breathing had returned to normal, she opened the suitcase in the cramped little space. Awkwardly she changed her stockings and exchanged the shoes with the loose heel for a pair of flat-heeled sandals. If she had to run again, she would at least be better equipped to do so. Her calves already ached with the unexpected exertion after more than a day in bed.

But perhaps she would not have to run again. She could stay here five minutes or an hour. Or three hours if she wished. And when she came out again, they would surely be gone. Bert would certainly loiter around the entrance, but after a time he would probably assume that she had come out among a crowd of other women and escaped his notice.

Or did she have unlimited time? There was no way of knowing what resources might lie behind Bert and the tall man. If they were the agents of an organization, they might easily have a woman in league with them, a woman who could come into the lavatory with impunity. And, once she left the security of the cubicle, she would be at the mercy of someone she wouldn't even recognize. Wildly she considered the possibility of one of the men coming into the lavatory disguised as a woman. The vision of Bert in skirts was somehow more horrible than the sight of him darting across the street had been.

She shuddered at the thought of his disguise, then began thinking logically. Disguise might act for her, not against her.

She pawed among the neatly packed clothing until she found a headscarf that she often wore when walking in the country. From her handbag she took a pair of dark spectacles and put them on. Then she knotted the scarf under her chin and pulled the top of it well forward until it almost met the top of the spectacles. The mackintosh still lay on top of the rest of her clothes. Standing up, she removed the sling from her left arm and awkwardly inserted it into a sleeve. The cast was bulky, but she finally succeeded in pushing it through the sleeve until her hand protruded, and then buttoned the coat to the chin. The conspicuous pink dress was totally covered, and the cast was invisible except for the stiffness of her arm. Even her shoes were different. Perhaps she could pass Bert unrecognized.

All that would betray her former appearance was the suitcase and that was impossible to disguise. She could scarcely hope to carry it under her coat. The combination of raincoat and sunglasses was already sufficiently strange without calling attention to it by a great protruding, pregnant mass beneath the mackintosh. There was nothing else to do: she must abandon the suitcase.

Carefully she locked the case, then pushed it back as far as she could to the side of the commode. Her name and home address were on the label attached to the handle, and with luck some honest person would forward it to her. Otherwise she would have to resign herself to the loss of her clothes.

As she opened the door of the cubicle, she saw a tired-looking old woman come out of one near her, carrying two heavy string bags of parcels. Briefly their eyes met. "Isn't it a heavenly day?" she fluttered, patting at her head scarf with her good hand.

To her relief the old woman smiled. "Beautiful. It was so pretty that I came all the way from Hammersmith to shop."

"And I came up from the country," Angela babbled. "I was afraid that it might rain, in spite of its being so lovely, and I wore my mac. It's too hot, and I wish I had left it at home."

"Still, you can't tell with a summer day. We may get a cool wind before evening, and you'll be glad of it."

Angela turned with the woman and walked beside her to the steps leading up into Leicester Square. Bert was probably waiting patiently outside the entrance.

"Those must be heavy, aren't they?" she asked, looking down at the string bags.

"I shouldn't have bought so much, but I don't get to the West End very often. But I can manage."

They had reached the foot of the stairs. "Here, let me help you," Angela said impulsively and seized one of the bags before the woman could protest. Together they went up, the old woman thanking her as she laboriously climbed the steps.

"Are you going towards Piccadilly Circus?" Angela asked.

"Yes, I'm going to get the bus there."

"I'll be glad to help you; I'm going that way, too."

"Thank you, dear." They had reached the top of the steps. Angela kept her head down, but she looked around ahead of her through the dark glasses. Nothing to be seen of Bert. Probably he was right behind her, but she dared not turn around.

The old woman chattered to Angela, and she responded in the lowest tones that she thought her companion could hear. There was no use in letting her voice give her away. It took the utmost in self-possession not to hurry the slow steps of the old woman, but she managed to restrain herself to a casual amble. At any moment Bert's hand might fall upon her shoulder. She felt her knees begin to shake with the effort of remaining calm. Everything depended upon that calm, but she knew how Lot's wife must have felt.

Past the last bit of green they went and crossed the street, still headed toward Piccadilly Circus. Suddenly she could stand the restraint no longer. She glanced behind her. Bert was looking curiously in her direction. He took a hesitant step or two after her. Her face must have betrayed her dismay, even at that distance, and he broke into a run.

"I'm so sorry, I must hurry," she had time to gasp as she handed the bag back to the startled old woman. Running more easily this time, she wound her way through the pedestrians. There was no time to see whether Bert was gaining. Ahead of her she could see Eros on his pedestal. At the entrance to the tube station, she darted left and raced down the steps and corridor to the booking hall. She was forced to a nervous walk in the crowd that filled it, but she made her way to the exit leading to the other side of Lower Regent Street.

Before she plunged into the exit corridor, she turned once more. Bert had just entered the booking hall. He was gaining on her, and he waved at her with what looked almost like gaiety.

By now her heart was pounding so loudly that she wondered whether the passers-by might hear it. She raced down the corridor, up the steps, and into the open once more.

She had not gone more than fifty steps when she saw a taxi

in the middle of the traffic, cruising slowly in search of fares. "Taxi!" she shouted in desperation. The driver gave her a nod, then headed for the curb. He had to wait for an opening as the agonizing seconds passed. She turned to look for Bert. He was thirty yards away, running as if breath were no problem for him.

Suddenly the taxi spurted forward and was at the curb. Before it had stopped, she grabbed the door handle and opened it. She threw herself inside and slammed the door. "Oxford Circus," she called to the driver, for it was the first name that came into her head. Slowly, painfully, the taxi edged away from the curb as Bert sprinted up to it.

The window of the taxi was open to the summer air. Before the taxi could move back into the traffic, Bert had put one hand on the top of the lowered glass, and with the other fumbled at the door handle. In one swift movement Angela lifted her left arm and smashed the cast down on his outspread fingers. He gave a howl of pain as he let go the handle and lurched backward. The taxi moved smoothly into the middle of the street and gathered speed. She looked through the rear window and saw Bert bent over double, shaking his injured hand.

"What's going on there, miss?" the driver called back.

"Oh, thank you so much for picking me up," she said. "That man had been bothering me, and I couldn't find a policeman." She let out a trembling breath that was not totally feigned. "It was terrible."

"Sorry for you, miss. But there's a lot of that kind of thing going on these days. It didn't used to be like that at all." He shook his head in satisfaction at the depravity of the world. "Oxford Circus, did you say?"

She knew she should not be so pleased with herself, but there was a morbid kind of satisfaction in knowing that she would not have been able to defend herself so well without the cast. He was paid back in his own kind. It was worth the new pain in her arm.

At Oxford Circus she could get the tube to Paddington. Without a suitcase she could manage it perfectly well. The next train would be at three-fifty-five. It was faster than the earlier one, with a change at Hatton. The only difficulty was that, if it were late getting into Stratford, dinner might be delayed, and the cook would probably be grumpy over that. But it couldn't be helped. She must remember to telephone about having missed the first train.

The taxi had nearly reached Oxford Circus when she realized that Bert had been very near and had probably heard her call out her destination to the driver. It would be difficult for him to get back there as quickly as she did, but she no longer wanted to take any chances. She needed somewhere to spend the hour or so before her train. A cinema in Oxford Street would give her the cover of darkness from the two men. But it would also give them cover. The thought of one of them coming near her in the dark decided her. She leaned forward. "Driver, I'm terribly sorry, but I wonder whether you could go to Trafalgar Square instead. The National Gallery." She would be surrounded by other people there, and she could at least see what was going on around her.

"You might have told me earlier," he grumbled.

"Yes, I know. But I was so upset by that man annoying me that I forgot about having to meet a friend at the National Gallery."

Mollified but still muttering about the inability of females to make up their minds, he turned at the next crossing to find his way through the maze of one-way streets. Oxford Circus, she thought, was really too near her flat in any case. They might return there in the hope of finding her again. Far better to keep completely away from the neighborhood.

After giving the driver a much larger tip than she had planned, she climbed the steps of the National Gallery and stood looking out at Trafalgar Square. Pigeons, bare feet, Nelson, the monumental tranquillity of Landseer, nursemaids, plumes of water blowing in the wind, Swedish student caps, the brooding calm of St. Martin-in-the-Fields. But behind the façade lay the violence that could so easily erupt when the disparate elements of a crowd in the Square turned into a protest meeting and then into a mob. Englishmen were apt to remark complacently that their capital was fortunately unlike the chaos of Paris or Tokyo or New York. Unlike they were, but beneath the surface of order lay cruelty and terror. She knew.

With horror she found herself speculating on possible escape routes in the great square before her. If she were to enter St. Martin's beneath the flamboyant coat of arms surmounting the main entrance, was there an inconspicuous side door by which she could creep out unseen, to run to Charing Cross Station or the crowds of the Strand? And the doors to the Gallery by which she stood were surely its only exits. Or had the thief who took the Goya made his escape through some other secret aperture?

She turned away from the scene beneath her and determinedly went inside. She was getting paranoid; even the events of that afternoon didn't excuse that sort of self-indulgence.

With amusement she remembered a passage in *The Way of All Flesh* in which Butler solemnly recommended to those who were distraught or nervous a long course of observation of the larger mammals in a zoo. Perhaps Rembrandt could do that for her. Probably not Greco. He was too fidgety. And Watteau was too minute. She needed larger mammals. Thank heaven, it wasn't the Tate Gallery. Turner's vast elemental disorders, his plunging seas and torn clouds: too much, in her present state. With relief she realized that she was beginning to play the frivolous kind of game with herself that presaged an inner balance. She laughed aloud, then saw the covertly apprehensive glance of an old man on a bench. He probably thought she was mad. Well, she wasn't. She might have been close to it a few minutes ago, but now she was perfectly all right, thank you.

Perhaps there was something in what Butler had said, but which pictures would he have prescribed for the recovery of mental equilibrium? Probably something marmoreal, she decided, with a slow, almost indiscernible heartbeat. Stubbs? Landseer? But they both painted animals, and it was human life that she needed to have readjusted. Besides, she wasn't at all sure that she could trust Butler about pictures. Music, so long as it was Handel, he understood, but not painting.

By the time she had entered the first gallery, she had forgotten Butler, but the compulsion to find repose was still strong. Not primitives. Too unresolved. Not French painters, on the whole. Not enough blood. She hesitated over Rembrandt's woman in white, lifting her skirt delicately over monumental legs as she waded into the water. Perhaps.

She stood longer before Uccello's *St. George and the Dragon.* The controlling geometry of the lance and wings. The confrontation between youthful saint and comic-strip dragon, the green of his scales receding before the pink of the maiden's draperies. Curious that she, in spite of the lance and wings, dominated the picture, not the saint or the dragon. And one didn't even know her name. Passivity overcoming force? Well, that had reference to her own plight, certainly.

Rubens. Giorgione. She walked on. Bronzino? Certainly marmoreal. Then she turned and walked swiftly through the galleries. One picture had been in the back of her mind ever since she entered. It was hardly fashionable to like Gainsborough, but every time she came into the museum she made a pilgrimage to his little painting of Mr. and Mrs. Robert Andrews.

The miraculously detailed skirt lay in deliberately casual blue folds over the formal green seat, so curiously placed in the miniature rural scene receding to the edges of the canvas. That was what made Gainsborough satisfying: his serene sense of balance. The urban seat against the chequered fields; the homely country beauty of the woman's face beneath the artifice of the dipping hat brim; her blue satin set off by the plain clothing of her husband; his rural stance contrasted with her crossed feet and quaintly ceremonious pose. Even, Angela thought, the ordered landscape, reduced to domesticity, was countered by the hint of natural violence in the shotgun he held.

She sighed. In the unlikely event that a grateful nation ever offered her a choice of the pictures in the museum, she was sure that she would hesitate for a long time over the Uccello. And take the Gainsborough.

With a stern return to practicality, she stood up. Plenty of time to get a taxi for Paddington and perhaps a cup of tea in the station. Perhaps she had made a fool of herself daydreaming over the pictures, but she had totally recovered her composure.

She found a taxi immediately outside the Gallery; since there was probably time, she thought briefly of going to the lavatory in Leicester Square to retrieve her suitcase, but she dismissed the idea almost as soon as it came to her. Surely Bert would realize that she had left the case behind, and he might take up his post there to await her return. "Paddington, please," she said.

The streets were crowded, and it was later than she had anticipated when she paid the driver. There was still a quarter of an hour before the train, but she wouldn't have time for tea. She bought her ticket and walked to the departure platform. A short queue was waiting to go through the entrance to the train. As she joined it, she hoped there would be a restaurant car; it seemed a long time since the jambalaya.

One by one the members of the queue presented their tickets for clipping and were waved off to the waiting train. She had splurged on a first-class ticket, so there should be no trouble getting a seat. There were only two men between her and the ticket collector when she heard a footstep beside her.

"A present for you, miss." It was the tall man. Automatically she held out her hand and took a small parcel with an envelope glued to it. "We've been trying to give it to you all afternoon. You shouldn't have hurried so much." He grinned sardonically as he turned away. "Pity about Bert. He didn't like it. He meant no harm. Have a good journey, miss." He was gone.

CHAPTER TWELVE

W HY EVER SHOULD I MIND?" Dame Millicent boomed. "I'm delighted you feel free to ask if you can come over here at any time." Good heavens, Angela was as nervous as a schoolgirl. She did hope the child wasn't getting sentimental about Michael. That wouldn't do at all. But it would explain why she was so skittish. However, she supposed the shock of the fractured arm was enough to make any normally sensible girl behave foolishly. "Your parents don't know how you got your arm broken, do they?"

"No. I asked Mike to tell them I had fallen down the stairs. I don't like lying to them, but Mother would have a fit if she knew. She's like a broody hen as it is. She seems to think I'm incapable of walking by myself. It's all I can do to keep her from going to the lavatory with me."

"That's not a bad thing." Mike frowned. "You shouldn't be by yourself any more than necessary. I know that this isn't London, but you ought to be careful. After what they did to you the other night, you mustn't take any chances."

"I think you're wrong," Angela said. "As I said, they don't really want to hurt me. They only want to frighten you away by threatening me." She ran her right hand over her cast. The arm had hurt occasionally since she hit Bert, but it was better now, and presumably she had not done it any harm. "But I must admit that I wasn't sure about that this afternoon."

"What happened?" Dame Millicent apologized mentally for her impatience about Angela. If the girl had had a fright, she might be excused for being nervous.

As deliberately and unexcitedly as she could, Angela told them of her encounter with Bert and the tall man. "But, you see," she said to Mike, "that proves that they didn't really want to hurt me, doesn't it? Frighten me, yes, but not harm me."

"But what," demanded Dame Millicent, "was in the package?" Perish the girl, would she never get to the point?

Angela flipped through her handbag and fished out a slip of paper. "This was the note."

Dame Millicent unfolded it deliberately. The lined paper had been ripped from a loose-leaf notebook. Printed in neat block letters was the short message. "Better listen to this," she read aloud from it. "before you take any further action." There was no salutation, no signature. "Listen to what?" she asked.

"A tape." Angela held up a flat box. "For a tape recorder."

"What does it say?" Florence Edwards had been silent, but she could contain her curiosity no longer.

"I don't know. I haven't had a chance to play it since I got back. Mother has hardly left my side. That's why I wanted to come over here." She looked at Mike. "And why I asked you to bring this in for me." She indicated the battered case that stood at her feet.

"Is that machine a tape recorder?" Dame Millicent had the sound of a woman who had never expected to have such a thing in her house.

"Yes. That's the terrifying thing. I don't see how they knew in the first place that I had one. The other thing is that it's an old-fashioned one I got when my uncle died, and it doesn't take standard-size tape. So I hardly ever use it any more. But this tape is the right size for it."

For the first time since Mike had met her, Angela looked desperately frightened, more so by far than she had when Bert pushed her arm down against the dining table in her flat. And then he recognized the cause of her fear. The one person who would know about the tape recorder was Jim, his own brother.

Dame Millicent cursed herself inwardly for being a thoughtless old woman. The poor child must be terrified at what the tape might contain. "May I help you with the machine?"

"No thanks," Angela said. "it's practically antediluvian, and I'm afraid no one could handle it who didn't know it intimately. But perhaps you would take off the lid, Mike, and plug in the cord."

Painstakingly she threaded the end of the tape into the second spool, then pressed a switch. The second spool jerked into action, and the tape snapped. "Damn," she said. The others were silent as she awkwardly repaired it with one hand. When she started the machine again, the tape held. There was a series of wheezes and whistles as she adjusted the volume, then the steady background hiss of the tape.

"Angela, this is Jim." His voice was surprisingly clear, Florence thought. The appearance of the tape recorder had prepared her for distortion. A pleasant voice, but it didn't have the vitality of Mike's. "I don't know how to begin except to say I'm sorry. This has probably hurt you a lot, and I don't like to think about that, but it was something I had to do." He not only lacked Mike's vitality; he sounded positively lackluster. But he must have been through a good bit himself. "You know that I love you, but there are times when it's necessary to give up personal relationships for something bigger. I don't know whether you can understand that or not, but it's true. And that is why I've had to hurt you. I've tried in every way I know to think of a way that we could be together, but it's impossible. I can't come back to England or the States, and you are much too English ever to be happy here."

Angela was sitting bolt upright in her chair, her right hand stroking her cast. The color had ebbed from her face, but her eyes were dry. Dame Millicent longed to go to her, but she knew that Angela would resent the offer of support as a sapping of her own strength.

"And so," the voice from the tape was saying, "the best thing is for you just to forget me. Make a new life without me." Several seconds of hissing tape intervened before he continued. "I hear that Mike is in England. Give him my apologies, please. And my love. And tell him that the best thing for him is to get . . ." He stopped as if short of breath. "To get to hell back home and not worry about me. And, whatever else you do, please don't try to find out anything about how I left England. It might be dangerous for you. Please don't. Goodbye, darling, and God bless you."

Then there was no more. The tears were flowing down Angela's face, but she made no gesture to wipe them away, and she sat as stiffly as before, seeming frozen in the chair. Mike was looking at her, his face under grim control, his emotions impenetrable. No one spoke as the tape hissed out its length.

The recorder was too out-of-date to switch off automatically, and the end of the tape flapped wildly around the second spool. Angela and Mike sat transfixed, listening to its noise without moving toward it. At last Dame Millicent went to the wall and switched it off. "Sorry," she said. "I didn't know how else to stop it." There was no answer.

She went to a table at the other end of the long drawing-room and poured out two glasses of brandy. "Thank you," Mike said flatly as she handed one to him. Angela reached automatically for a glass without speaking or looking up, but instead of drinking she held it in her hand as if she had forgotten it.

"It was your brother's voice, wasn't it?" asked Florence, although she knew the answer before she spoke. At the risk of pain,

Angela had to be jolted out of her state of shock. Mike nodded.

Angela brushed at her tears and took a sip of brandy. "Yes, it was Jim," she said in a monotone. "I'd know his voice anywhere." She shook her head back and forth slowly. "He sounded so terribly tired. He must have gone through hell."

"At least," said Florence, "we know that he is alive, and that's a great deal to be thankful for. I'm sure we all wondered about that until now." She was aware of how cold her comfort was, but the horrible silence that had fallen before had somehow to be broken up.

"Yes," said Mike brutally, "we know that he was alive when he made that tape. We don't know that he is now."

Angela still sounded dazed as she spoke. "I don't understand it. I mean, it doesn't all fit together."

"Why not?" Dame Millicent snapped more quickly than she had intended.

"Because he called me darling." She smoothed her handkerchief in her lap, pushing out each point carefully. Then she folded it into a neat square. "I don't suppose he had called me that more than two or three times in all the while I knew him. It was a kind of joke with us. You see, the second time I saw him, he called me that by accident. That is, he meant it, but he didn't intend to say it. Do you understand? I suppose I looked surprised, and then I asked him if he always did that. He laughed and said he only called girls darling when he intended to marry them. But he didn't say it any more. Usually he called me Funny-face when he was being affectionate. Or Pops. That was short for poppet." She gave a forced little smile. "I know how silly it sounds in cold blood, but that's how it was.

"Anyway, I think the only other time he ever called me darling was the night that we decided to get married. We laughed about it, and he—he said that he had made up his mind to marry me the second time he saw me." The tears had begun running down her cheeks again, but she left them unchecked. "So, you see, it seems so much worse that he should say it now that —now that he isn't going to marry me."

"The bastard!" Mike spoke so softly that Dame Millicent scarcely understood him.

"Don't you dare say that!" Angela's voice sparkled with anger. "I don't know why he did it, but he wouldn't have if he hadn't thought it was necessary. I loved him before, and I love him now, whatever he did." Her eyes snapped. "Don't you dare say it again."

Nor would he, Dame Millicent thought. At least the interchange had brought Angela out of her lethargy. She would make it now. "You don't really believe that, do you, Michael?"

"No, I don't. I know there has to be some explanation. But I couldn't bear seeing Angela put through the wringer." He turned to Angela. "I'm sorry. I really didn't mean it."

She got up from her chair, walked to Mike, and put her hand on his shoulder. "I know. Your saying that was just your way of expressing what I did by crying. Forget it, Mike."

"Very well, then. Let's put on our thinking caps. Surely there is enough intelligence in this room to figure out the possibilities that face us. Let's all put our shoulders to the wheel." Dame Millicent hated assuming her low-comedy role of Deirdre Desiree, but it was sometimes necessary. Once, she reflected, she had been able to make the transition at will. The difficulty was that as one grew older, it became harder to distinguish between the role and the reality. Perhaps she really was becoming a silly old woman. At least she knew when she was using clichés. Thinking caps and shoulders to the wheel, indeed! Well, she could make Angela and Michael think less about their own emotions. "Let's list the possibilities. I'll put them down on paper. That's what I always do when I'm writing my novels.

"First of all, there is the possibility that the tape means just what it says, that Jim wants you both to forget him. And I suppose we'd have to add then that he defected of his own volition." She held up her hand at Angela. "Don't interrupt, my dear. I'm speaking of remote possibilities only."

"We've been over this too often," Mike said wearily. "Angela doesn't believe, and I don't believe, and I doubt that anyone here believes that Jim defected without pressure. Scratch that one."

"Very well, I'll cross that one out." She wrote furiously, then looked up again. "The second possibility is that he didn't go to

Russia voluntarily, and that he was somehow forced into making the recording. Right?"

Florence Edwards considered. "If that were so, do you think that he might have said 'darling' so that Angela would realize that he didn't mean what had gone before?" She looked at Dame Millicent, who was scowling with concentration. "Well, it is possible, isn't it?"

"I know that I'd like to believe it," said Angela, "and perhaps that keeps me from seeing what is wrong with the suggestion. All the same, it would explain his saying 'darling.' Whatever else he might be, Jim isn't ever deliberately cruel, and he would have known how it would hurt to hear him call me that. If he were forced into making the recording, that would be like him, to try to send me a secret message in it."

"Angela," said Mike gently, "I know that would be like Jim, but I don't suppose he would be free to say what he wanted. Surely they would tell him exactly what he had to say."

"I know you are being cautious because you don't want me to be disappointed, but I still think he might have added one word. They wouldn't think there was anything strange about his wanting to call me that." Angela set her jaw stubbornly, and Mike gave up. No use in taking away any comfort she might have.

Something kept ticking away uncomfortably in her mind, but Dame Millicent couldn't isolate it. Something about the message itself. She did hope that her memory was not failing. Well, perhaps it would come to her later. Meanwhile, she ought to carry on with the possibilities as they presented themselves. The difficulty was that it was so hard to sort them out. "What do you think we ought to take up next?" she asked, hoping for help.

"There is one thing we might consider," said Mike, "although it isn't very pleasant. How do you suppose they could have forced him to send a message unless he agreed with it? He sounded terribly tired, as Angela says, and I suppose they might have just talked him into it. Hypnotized him or something of the sort, or told him it would be better for everyone concerned. He might have believed that, even if the bit about personal relationships not being so important as bigger things doesn't make sense.

At least not for Jim."

"But then why would he have agreed to saying that it would be better not to inquire into how he left?" Angela asked. "That wouldn't be like him either. I think you're shying away from saying what we're all thinking: he might have been drugged or tortured into making that recording. It's awful to think of, but there's no use in refusing to consider it."

"Surely the most probable explanation is the simplest one, isn't it?" Florence Edwards's eyes were sparkling as she tried to figure out all the possibilities. She hated to admit it to herself, when Angela and Mike were going through hell, but it was terribly exciting. "You said yourself that they broke your arm to get Mike to go away, not because they wanted to hurt you. If your safety is important to Mike, think how much more important it is to his brother." Oh, dear, she hoped that hadn't been tactless. "All they would have to do is to tell Jim that they would hurt you if he didn't make the recording. There was something about it just before the end, wasn't there? I don't remember the words exactly, though." She felt a bit crestfallen that she couldn't remember.

Thank heaven for a good memory! Dame Millicent recalled now what she had been trying to think of before. "Why don't we play the end of the recording again and see what the words actually were. Angela, my dear, if you don't mind, could you put on the last bit again?"

Angela rethreaded the spools, reversed the tape part way, then started it playing again: ". . . is in England. Give him my apologies, please. And my love. And tell him that the best thing for him is to get . . . to get to hell back home and not worry about me. And, whatever else you do, please don't try to find out anything about how I left England. It might be dangerous for you. Please don't." She shut it off before she had to hear his last words to her.

Florence nodded vehemently. "That's what I meant, his saying it would be dangerous." She felt rather annoyed. Dame Millicent was paying no attention at all. "Did you hear, Millicent?"

"Mmm. Yes. I dare say you are right. Mmm. How long had

Jim been in this country, Michael?"

"About three years. Why?" It was unlike Dame Millicent to be rude to Mrs. Edwards.

"And in that time he hadn't lost his Amer—I mean, he hadn't begun to pick up English ways of speech, had he? I didn't know him well, but I should have said that he still sounded very American indeed. Wouldn't you, Angela?"

"Yes, but I don't see that there's anything wrong with that." She sounded annoyed.

"Of course not, of course not. Not a thing in the world. And no doubt in time he would have learned. But I think he **was** trying to tell you that what he was saying weren't his own words, and that someone else had written them. Didn't you notice?" The faces around her remained blank. "He said, 'the best thing for him is to get,' and then he stopped. He was calling attention to what followed. And then he went on, 'to get to hell back home.' He even repeated 'to get,' to emphasize what he was about to say.

"When I was teaching in America, I was naturally interested in the differences between American speech and its proper English forms, so I spent a good bit of time listening to the idiom. Most instructive. Most. Now, one of the phrases that interested me was a very common one among your countrymen, Michael. It was 'Get the hell out.' Of course, American pronunciation, with its—its somewhat imprecise quality, isn't always easy for us to follow. I had assumed until then that what they were saying was 'Get *to* hell out,' and that is the way I should have said it. Not, mind you, that I'd say it, even if I had the occasion. All the same, that's the way I thought I had heard it."

She stopped. "Oh, dear, this doesn't seem as clear when I tell it as when I think about it. Still, perhaps you'll understand. Well, the thing is that "Get the hell out' doesn't really make much sense, does it? Once I had noticed it, I was fascinated by the phrase. And, when I got back home, I happened to mention it to friends of mine who were interested in such things. Curiously enough, they all had the same mistaken idea that I had had. Presumably the influence of the cinema. I fancy that American actors don't speak well because they have never had training in classical drama."

She put her hand to her head. "I suppose that isn't relevant, though, is it? But what is relevant is that your brother or any other American would say, 'Get the hell,' and it would be so inbred that he wouldn't change it, no matter how long he had lived here. And, when he paused, he was trying to draw one's attention to the fact that he was reading a prepared speech." She stopped, obviously slightly confused. "You do understand, don't you?"

"You're right," Mike said slowly. "And I didn't even notice it. Thank heaven you did."

"Now that you mention it," Angela said, "I know that I've often heard Jim use the phrase."

Dame Millicent beamed at their agreement, then a look of gloom settled over her face. "But that means, of course, that we can't trust anything else that he said. Not one word."

"Yes we can," said Angela. "One word. Darling."

CHAPTER THIRTEEN

MIKE SWUNG HIS ARMS to warm himself. Not his idea of midsummer, although it hadn't seemed to bother the Hethereges. He looked at Dame Millicent whirling the tractor around, her raincoat unbuttoned as if she were in New York on a steamy August day, rather than in this bleak, wet, windswept farmyard in Warwickshire. He wondered how many generations it took to develop such bland obliviousness to the weather.

He had put on two undershirts that morning, but it didn't seem to help much. Creeping down to the dining room for breakfast, he had taken a furtive look at the thermometer in the front hall. Forty-eight frigid degrees! To be honest about it, someone had turned on an electric stove in the dining room, but it was a single undernourished strand of wire that had no noticeable effect on the temperature of the air.

Moving his toes up and down in his shoes to keep them from frostbite, he had greedily eaten his bacon and eggs, then held his coffee cup in both hands to restore the circulation. But Peregrine read *The Times* imperturbably, and Dame Millicent absent-mindedly unfastened another button at the neck of her dress as she worked resolutely through her morning's mail. Only Florence Edwards seemed pinched and white, as though her blood were slowly congealing. And even she was wearing a heavy sweater for which Mike would cheerfully have given a gelid right arm. His own limited wardrobe had not been chosen with this kind of emergency in mind.

At last, driven to extremity by the blast that stirred the carpet, he had ventured to say to the table at large, "I wonder whether you knew that the front door was open." There was no response for some time, then Peregrine put down his newspaper and shuffled to the window in his slippers. Intently he peered out of the glass over his spectacles before he returned to the table. "It's quite all right," he said placidly as he picked up *The Times* again. "The front gate's locked."

And now Mike stood in a howling wind, the rain forcing itself through his raincoat while he watched Dame Millicent and the farmer trying out the new tractor and mowing machine. In the cab of the tractor Dame Millicent was steering them around in enormous erratic circles. Her driving, he realized, was even more capricious aboard the great farm machine than it was in her tiny car, but that clearly bothered her not a whit. "Pretty little thing," she bellowed over her shoulder to the farmer, who was operating the mowing attachment, dragged pitiably behind the tractor. He stood on a little platform presiding at the controls. The lever under his right hand operated a great jointed steel arm, and his left hand turned a wheel that controlled the angle of the steel blades whirling at the end of the arm.

Dame Millicent took one more turn around the farmyard, her steering somewhat impaired by her insistence on looking backward at the farmer and the mowing machine. Mike watched her cautiously; she would probably run her juggernaut over him the moment he averted his eyes.

She whirled the tractor to a stop in a puddle near the gate. So tall were the wheels, so cushioned the ride that she remained oblivious of the steel bucket she had just flattened. Nimbly she leapt down into the water and shouted to the farmer, "Now let me try the mower, Scroggs."

"Better not, Miss Millicent," he replied sourly. "Not today, in all the rain. Come back someday when it's fine." He looked apprehensively at the fruit trees at the edges of the yard, clearly afraid that their last day had come if she were turned loose with the mower.

They began a friendly argument about the price of barley, and Mike stopped listening. He hoped Scroggs would soon agree to whatever she was proposing, so that she would come back to the car. Probably the farmer would give in before long; he was already looking cowed by the volley of words. Mike envied Iseult, lying in comfort on the back seat of the car. No fool, that dog. She had taken one disbelieving look out of the door, then jumped back up on the seat and curled into a warm ball. He would have joined her were it not for an obscure feeling that he would be letting his own country down.

At last the farmer began nodding in agreement. In a moment Dame Millicent made her farewell to him and turned toward the car. "So glad you saw the light of reason," she called sunnily over her shoulder. "Goodbye, Scroggs." Mike waved goodbye and leapt with alacrity into the car, not even waiting to help Dame Millicent.

"Mind if I turn on the heater?" he asked as she started the engine.

"Do, by all means," she said as she rolled down a window. "I do hope Scroggs will make good use of that tractor. He's the best tenant I've got on any of my farms, and I helped him buy it. But he's a bit cautious, and he may not take full advantage of it. I wish I had more time; I should love to drive it for him.

Disdainful of the potholes pitting the lane, the car roared away, lurching up and down in imminent danger to its suspension. Suddenly Dame Millicent slammed on the brakes. Directly across the lane, on her side of the car, stood the largest manure heap Mike had ever seen. It must be at least thirty feet long and ten feet high, he decided. Even in the rain it exhaled steam and an overpowering stench that made Iseult stir uneasily on the back seat. Talk about pollution in the cities, he thought.

Dame Millicent inhaled deeply. "Lovely! There's nothing nicer than a good dunghill." She pronounced it "dungle." "It's the sign of an efficient farmer. Good man, Scroggs, although he is a bit stubborn." She took another deep breath and regretfully put the car into motion again.

"If it's not a nuisance," Mike said, "I'll go into Stratford with you. Then you won't have to take me back home. Besides, I'd not mind doing a little shopping myself. I thought perhaps I'd buy a cashmere sweater. They're so much cheaper here than they are at home." Cashmere my eye, he thought; he'd buy the heaviest Irish fisherman's pullover he could find.

"Delighted to have you." As the car crashed from crag to crag in the lane, she fished in her purse with one hand, pulled out a cigarette, and fitted it into a long holder. She pushed in the lighter on the dashboard and waited for it to pop out again. When nothing happened, she casually let go the steering wheel and tugged at the lighter with both hands. Mike made a grab for the wheel and steered them safely past a hole two feet deep.

"Thank you," she said when she had lighted her cigarette. "I do wish Scroggs would repair this lane. It's a positive menace."

Shortly they were on the road to Market Doddington. "My own shopping doesn't amount to much. I want to get a case of bourbon. Watkins at our local doesn't run to what he regards as a flight of exotic fancy. Actually, of course, what I get in Stratford really isn't bourbon, it's Canadian whiskey. But I have to make do." She stopped, as if unsure what her starting point had been. "Oh, yes. What I was leading up to is that I'll not take long. I shouldn't mind at all waiting for you, but a man ought not be rushed when he's buying a sweater. Perhaps you'd rather I left you and then came back for you about twelve-thirty. Iseult would be glad of the extra drive. I've got a number of things to tend to at home this morning."

"That's very kind of you to offer, but it's far too much trouble. Couldn't I take a bus? Otherwise, I'll come back with you."

"There won't be a bus until after lunch, I'm afraid. The whole transport system in this country is being ruined by the government. There used to be a bus every hour. Now there are only three a day. It's monstrous." She was off on what Mike decided must be a practically treasonous diatribe against the government.

She interrupted herself to point out of the window. "That's the old American air base. Nether Otford." The steel fence surrounding the air field was the only part of it that looked in reasonable repair. Beyond it he could see hangars, their doors dangling askew, windowpanes long since shattered. At one end of the field a little group of Nissen huts had fallen in, and grass sprouted through the cracks between the sheets of corrugated steel.

"Not very big, is it?" He could see only one runway.

"That was the trouble with it. It couldn't handle the big planes, and there wasn't any room to expand. I hated it when it was in operation. The noise was unspeakable when the planes were taking off. But I must say that I think I preferred it that way. It's an eyesore now, and it keeps a lot of good farming land from being used."

"How long since it was used?"

"Eight or ten years, I should think."

"I believe the landlord at the White Hart mentioned it the other night." The rank weeds around the old runway faded from sight. "I've been thinking. The easiest thing would be for me simply to stay in Stratford and come out on the afternoon bus, if that wouldn't upset lunch. Would it be inconvenient for you?" Visions of pints of beer by the roaring fire of a pub floated through his mind.

"Not at all, if you'd like it. If you are going to stay, you might even be able to get a ticket for the afternoon performance at the theatre. I think they're doing *Timon* today."

Given a choice, Mike would not have picked *Timon of Athens* to while away an afternoon, but he was sure that he would be considerably warmer in the theatre than in the drawing room of Cuthberts. Even with his new sweater. Better still, he could go to a nice steamy movie. "Would there be a bus after the theatre?"

"Six o'clock. It'll get you back in plenty of time for dinner."

Market Doddington was a mile and a half from Lower Doddington, on the main road to Stratford, along which they had driven in their visit earlier in the week to the Centre. The road by which they were approaching the village today ran along a low ridge. As they came out of a stretch of trees, the village lay spread out before them. Mike wished that they could stop for a moment to look at it, but he was afraid that if he were to suggest such a thing Dame Millicent might jam on the brakes dead in the middle of the road. It wasn't worth it.

"There's a lay-by ahead. Why don't we have a look at the village? It's a pretty sight." She looked sideways at him as she spoke. "And a good view of the Hall." The woman must be a mindreader.

From the gravel semicircle where she parked the car, they could see the length of the road on which they had been driving, as it wound down the hill, along the side walls of the park, and finally made a junction with the main Stratford road, on which the Hall and the park fronted. It must have been a beautiful house, he thought, before the modern laboratory had been built onto it at the rear, cutting off the splendid view to the water meadows and the river that meandered through them. And from the front it still maintained a diminished elegance. It was a rectangular Queen Anne house, the warm pink of the brick keeping its austere outlines from looking cold. Around the entire top ran a raised frieze hiding the lead roof from ground-level view.

A formal house, and once the park had been formal too. The main drive led in a straight parting of the grass to the gatehouse. Mike could see the guard dogs churning in their pen. Equidistant from the main gates, near the wall along the main road, stood two smaller houses, their façades identical so far as he could tell. But, from where he stood, he could see that one of them was only half as deep as the other. One of them, the old dower house, he knew was where Plymson lived. Or had lived. There were half a dozen wooden buildings, one story high, strewn around the sides of the main house without any order or symmetry that he could perceive.

The park had been rectangular, too, with a high wall along

the road, which turned to enclose the house, extending on either side of it down to the river. But it looked as if the meadows no longer formed part of the park. A short distance behind the laboratory a high steel fence had been erected to connect the two great arms of wall. There were cows in the meadows, but they were separated from the house by the fence and the slanting rows of barbed wire that leaned out from its top. The barbed wire matched that which had been erected on top of the walls. Not very hospitable.

"Don't the water meadows belong to the Centre?" he asked.

"Indeed they do, but I wish they didn't. They are going to sell them for a development. The District Council won't do anything to stop them. Barbaric. I hope that Plymson's death may put a spanner in the works."

"Which was his house?"

She pointed. "The farther one. It was the dower house. The smaller one is where Teddy Doddington's agent lived. I think it's been made into flats. Plymson's assistant lives there, I believe. It makes my blood boil to see what they've done." She looked at her watch. "Time we were going before it begins to boil in earnest."

An hour later Mike was feeling distinctly better. When he came out of the shop, the rain had stopped, but the uplift of his spirits had begun before that, at the moment when he had pulled the bulky sweater over his head, drawn his jacket over it, and covered them both with his raincoat. To be honest, he was beginning to wonder whether the sweater wasn't just a trifle too heavy. But better a little sweat than death by exposure.

He must be getting used to Stratford, for he was no longer so annoyed by it as he had been in the past. And it was pleasant to have several hours ahead of him with no need to worry about anyone else. He realized that it was the first time he had been alone for any length of time since his first visit to Stratford. Thank heaven, he didn't have the flu now.

The rain had stopped, but it wasn't a day for the Dirty Duck, and anyway it wouldn't be much fun without—well, without a companion. Angela's outburst the night before had made it clear where her affections lay. That was right, too. He bought a sandwich and beer at a pub and thought about Angela and Jim as he ate.

The tape proved there was something about Jim's disappearance that could still threaten whoever had sent him to Russia. Whoever that was must still be in England, or the exposure would mean nothing. Unless it was Plymson. He had died two days before, and the tape would surely have been on its way to England by then. Still, why should the tall man have been so anxious to give it to Angela after his death if Plymson were the man who was being protected? There didn't seem to be a very good answer to that one.

And it was equally clear that Jim was still under some kind of compulsion. Would the rest of his life be led in this way, or would he capitulate in time and cooperate voluntarily? It would be the only way ever to have a moderately free life in Russia, even if that freedom didn't include leaving the country. If he decided to cooperate eventually, Mike couldn't really blame him much. A man lives only once. And Jim was a damned good chemist. If he cooperated, he'd probably be given a reasonable job.

When he finished his lunch, he realized guiltily that he hadn't even inquired about tickets for *Timon*. He had intended to, although he felt no enthusiasm for the play, but he had totally forgotten after passing a cinema advertising the revival of two Marx Brothers films. Groucho rather than Timon any day.

It was five o'clock when he left the cinema. The sun had come out, and he put his raincoat over his arm. An hour before the bus, with plenty of time to wander around the town. He drifted along the streets, looking in windows. He was about to turn away from a display of cameras when he remembered that Mrs. Edwards had said she was out of color film. He could save her a trip by buying some now.

As the woman behind the counter wrapped the film, he looked casually around the shop. Originally there had been two shops, now made into one by a large doorway knocked through the wall. He looked through the connecting doorway at a bewildering array of radios, tape recorders, and record players.

"Excuse me," he said impulsively, "have you got tape for a Turnbull-Elliott tape recorder?"

"Certainly," she said, handing him the film. "What model number, please?"

"I don't know the number. It's an old one, though. I believe the name on it was Verisone. Could that be right?"

She looked surprised. "There is a Verisone model, but it's certainly an old one. Probably more than twenty years old. They changed the size of the tape on the Turnbull-Elliotts a long time ago. That one took an odd size. I'll have to ask whether we've got any." She opened a door at the back of the shop and shouted up a stairway. "Roy!" Then she repeated Mike's request. "Just a minute," she said when she turned around. "My husband is coming down."

There were steps on the stairs, and a middle-aged man appeared. "We've got three boxes of tape for that model, sir. They're the last we'll be getting. They've gone out of production. If I were you, sir, I'd buy all three. You'll have a difficult time finding more after this."

"One will be enough," said Mike. "When did they stop making them?"

"Two or three years ago, if I remember correctly. We've had these around for some time. Not many requests for them nowadays. Most people prefer getting a new machine that takes standard tape. But it was a good machine. For its day, I mean. All superseded now, though." He looked as if he regretted the passing of time. "Curious you should ask for this. I sold another roll not long ago. Four or five days, I suppose. It was the first request for one I had had in a year or two."

"I wonder if it could have been someone buying it for my aunt with whom I'm staying. She's a pianist, and she uses the tape recorder when she's practicing." Mike's invention ran out.

The man passed his hand over his chin. "I'm afraid I've forgotten who it was, sir."

"Could it have been a tall man? Rather narrow face. He usually wears a checked coat."

"Sorry, I've completely forgotten. We serve so many people, you see, sir, that it's hard to remember. But you can bring this back if your aunt has got a sufficient supply." Then he added hastily, "So long as it's not opened, of course."

Mike had to hurry to reach the ironmonger's shop before it closed. There he bought wire cutters and a pocket flashlight. The queue was already forming in the bay for the bus back to Lower Doddington. So far as he could tell, he knew no one else in the queue.

He sat by himself on the lower deck of the bus. It seemed to him that the driver stopped at every crossroad they passed. The trip to Lower Doddington took little more than half an hour, he knew, but he didn't see how the schedule could be maintained at this creeping pace. He wanted to be back at Cuthberts in time for a couple of drinks before dinner at seven-thirty, and it would take him five minutes to walk there from the bus. And he would have to change.

The bus pulled in at a stop on the edge of Market Doddington. Not more than another five or ten minutes now. He looked out of the window without curiosity at the car passing the bus. Without curiosity at first, but not after he had seen the driver of the car. It was Stevenson.

The bus started again, but it did not pick up much speed, for there was another stop in the middle of Market Doddington. Mike pulled the cord, and when the bus stopped before the Spread Eagle, he got off with two women who were carrying shopping bags.

CHAPTER FOURTEEN

I T'S AN INTERMINABLE PLAY, I must admit, but surely it isn't as long as all that." Dame Millicent brandished her glass of bourbon at Angela. "I've seen *Timon* only once, and it seemed as if hours, absolute hours were passing. All the same, I think he might have caught the six-o'clock bus."

"Rude. Damned rude. All young men are rude nowadays. That man at Market Doddington who was here for a drink. Telling me his name was Plymson, then claiming it was Applethwaite. And taking a drink for himself out of the sherry bottle. Damned rude." Peregrine picked up the cushions of the sofa and looked carefully under them as if searching for Mike. "But I'm surprised at Templeman—at Edwards, that is. Thought he had better manners. But let's not wait for dinner any longer."

"Really, Peregrine, you are getting impossible. He never said his name was Plymson. And I'm sure Michael must have a perfectly good reason for being late. He's a well-bred young man."

Peregrine snorted. "Perfectly good reason, eh? I'll wager he found some young woman in Stratford. Forgot the time. That's what happened." He looked at Angela. "Sorry to have you hear this sort of talk, m'dear. But it's the way young men are. Pity, but it's the truth."

"The trouble with you, Peregrine," said Dame Millicent, "is that you led an exemplary youth, and now you want to attribute to the young people of today everything you regret that you missed. You wish that you were one of those virile young men in my novels, with gray eyes, cleft chin, and hair starting above the open neck of his shirt. Envy, sheer envy."

"Would it be all right," intervened Florence Edwards tactfully, "if I were to call the theatre at Stratford, to find out when the performance finished this afternoon?"

She came back from the telephone with a look of puzzlement on her face. "They said it was over before five-thirty. That should have given him plenty of time to get the bus, shouldn't it?"

"I don't like it," said Angela. "Those men said that they hadn't tried to kill him by running him down, and it's true that they didn't hurt him when they were in my flat, but they may be more desperate, now that they realize he isn't going to leave as they asked. They seemed to have no trouble in tailing him before, and I'm afraid they could easily have followed him today. It's worrying."

"I think you are unduly nervous about Michael," said Dame Millicent. "I'm positive there was no one after us when we were going to the farms this morning, and if they hadn't followed us then, I don't see how they could have picked us up later. No, I feel sure no one was 'tailing' us, as you say."

Angela looked singularly unconvinced. "What is so damnable is that we can't just lift the telephone and tell the police that Mike is missing."

"We could," Dame Millicent said, "but what we couldn't tell them is who he is, and that is the one fact that would get them really interested. If they didn't know who he was, they would probably tell us just not to worry, that he would come back soon." She laid a hand on Angela's cast. "Try not to think about it too much. I'm not so unsympathetic as I seem. But fretting won't help. Let's have our dinner, and if he hasn't come by the time we finish, we'll take some kind of action then."

It was after nine when they finished their coffee. "Haven't we waited long enough?" Angela asked. "We've got to do something. There's no telling what may have happened to Mike."

"All right. Florence, you must come along. And I know that you'll want to come, Angela. How about you, Peregrine?"

He looked up, over his glasses. "I'll come if you need me. Otherwise, I'd like to watch *The Con Men*. Hear it's a good program."

"Have a good time. We'll not need you." Dame Millicent and her brother, Angela realized, were far more fond of each other than the surface of their bickering suggested. "We'll take Iseult instead."

Angela shared the back seat of the car with Iseult, while Florence Edwards sat next to Dame Millicent. "Do you really want me to come?" Mrs. Edwards asked. "I'm afraid I'll only be in the way." She sounded wistful, as if she felt that she should offer to stay at home but hoped that the offer would not be accepted.

"Not very maternal of you, Florence. Don't forget that you are supposed to be Michael's mother. It would be most peculiar if you didn't go personally to the police when your son disappeared."

The stage, Angela decided, had lost a fine actress when Mrs. Edwards settled down to domesticity in Blandinsville. She had admired her performance playing opposite Plymson at Dame Millicent's sherry party. Tonight in another role she was equally convincing. "I'm sorry I've got to bother you," she was saying to the officer in the Stratford police station. "It's my boy. My boy Mike. I worry a lot about him when we're away from home like this."

"What's the trouble?" The policeman was obviously as easy a prey as Plymson had been. Angela was afraid he might pat Mrs. Edwards on the hand, touched by her maternal vulnerability.

"I suppose I shouldn't worry so much about him. He's a big boy. He's thirty-two." Angela saw the policeman's eyebrows shoot up, and presumably Mrs. Edwards realized that she was overplaying it. "He can take care of himself, I know, but I get nervous when he's not around. I've never been this far from Blandinsville before, and I need him to take care of me."

"How long has he been missing?"

She looked at her watch. "Three hours. He should have been back in Lower Doddington at six-thirty. And it's almost nine-thirty. Late."

The policeman was beginning to look considerably less concerned. "Well, perhaps he'll come back when the pubs close. Lots of boys—men—like to have a pint or two by themselves."

"I'm afraid he might have found some young woman in Stratford and forgotten the time." She looked over her shoulder at Angela. "Sorry to have you hear this kind of talk, my dear. But it's the way young men are." She turned back to the policeman. "I'm sure a good-looking young man like you knows about that. But you're positive you haven't had any report about his being found? There are lots of hit-and-run drivers around these days."

"Quite sure. We'll let you know if we hear anything. But I imagine you'll find him with his feet up when you get back."

Mrs. Edwards and Angela walked out the door together. "Don't you think you were sailing a bit near the wind with that imitation of Mr. Hetherege? I was afraid that either Dame Millicent or I might laugh aloud."

"Sorry." Florence looked contrite. "I'm afraid I have a strong streak of vulgar comedy in me. At least, it worked."

Behind them, at the desk, Angela could hear Dame Millicent saying, "You mustn't worry about her. She's—well, she's a bit oversensitive about her son. I think many American women are. She insisted on coming here, and I could hardly refuse to bring her." In a stage whisper quite as carrying as her previous words, she added, "I think she's just the faintest bit neurotic." Probably, Angela decided, deliberate repayment for the imitation of Peregrine.

"Anyway," Mrs. Edwards said complacently as she got back into the car, "I did find out that the police had no record of his being injured or anything of that sort. So perhaps that excuses my being a ham. And now what?"

"The bus station, I think," said Dame Millicent. "And perhaps I should make the inquiries there."

The desk was closed when they arrived at the bus station, but as Dame Millicent entered, she met a girl locking a door behind her. Grudgingly the girl admitted that she served behind the desk during the day. Dame Millicent asked whether she could remember Mike's buying a ticket.

"I'm afraid," she answered in a genteel voice as she patted her platinum hair, "I can't be of any help to you. Tickets are purchased on the bus." She polished her nails on a none-too-clean sleeve and prepared to turn away.

"The man about whom I am asking was an American. I thought perhaps he wouldn't have realized that he could buy his ticket on the bus, and that he might have tried to buy one here. He's tall—"

"I'm afraid," the girl repeated in a bored voice, careful of her vowels, "I can't be of any help to you. I really can't remember all the members of the public who come in here."

Not surprising, Dame Millicent thought, if you don't even look at them when they speak. "Thank you," she said and turned to go back to the car.

"Pardon." It was the girl's voice again, with a slight note of what might have been urgency had she been less self-conscious. She held up a hand at Dame Millicent. "Actually, if it really is important, you might talk to the conductor. His bus should be arriving back in five minutes."

Dame Millicent had already considered, then rejected, asking about the conductor, for she didn't like calling too much attention to Mike before they knew that he was really in danger. This made it easy.

The conductor turned out to be considerably more helpful than the girl. He remembered quite distinctly that an American of Mike's description had boarded the bus and bought a ticket, and when Dame Millicent suggested Lower Doddington as his destination, the conductor agreed that it was probably where Mike had asked to go. No, he didn't exactly remember seeing Mike leave the bus, although he had presumably got off at the church in Lower Doddington, for there were several other passengers who got off there. Perhaps he would remember the others if he saw them, but he couldn't recall them offhand. He wasn't normally on that run, and he didn't know the regulars. Sorry, but that was the best he could do.

"I think the wisest course is simply to go home," Dame Millicent said as she came back to the car. "He may have come back by now. And, since we know that he got as far as Lower Doddington, there isn't much use in staying here."

"Does he know anyone else in the village?" asked Angela. "The rector, or the Hayleys, perhaps?"

"Not well enough to drop in on. I don't think he has met anyone except at the sherry party last week when he met you. Your parents, of course, but he doesn't know them better than he does the others. I can't think where he could have gone."

It was nearly ten-thirty by the clock of Lower Doddington church when they turned off the main road and down the narrower one that led to Cuthberts. As they approached the White Hart, they could see half a dozen cars parked outside. "Looks like a good night for Watkins," said Dame Millicent. "His custom has been falling off lately, and I have been afraid that he might have to give up the lease. I like to have a good pub in the village. It keeps the young men out of trouble. Beer and darts are better for them than haring around on those unspeakable motorcycles."

They had almost passed the pub when Angela drew in her breath sharply. "Oh!" she said.

Dame Millicent slammed on the brakes, shaking Iseult off the back seat. "Whatever is the matter, child?"

"I'm sorry. Just for a moment I thought I saw the car that those two men drive. You know, the one that nearly ran us down in Stratford, and that they were in when I saw them in London. But I must be mistaken."

"Which one?" Dame Millicent turned around to look back at the pub.

"The one by the gate. It's a Vauxhall, and it looks as if it were blue. But that's silly. There must be thousands of blue Vauxhalls, and I'm not even sure in this light that it's blue. I think I must be losing my grip ever since that day in London. Sorry I alarmed you."

"It ought to be easy enough to find out," said Mrs. Edwards. "Why don't we just go into the pub and see if the men are there?"

"Women's liberation hasn't gone as far as that in England, Florence. There's no law against our going in, but if we did, we'd certainly be the only women in the place." She considered. "The only ones of our . . . of our sort. And we'd attract a great deal more attention than I think is desirable."

"Couldn't I go in alone, then? I know that Angela can't go in because the men would recognize her if they are there. But I'm American, and anyone would realize that I didn't know women aren't supposed to be there."

"Not a chance. I don't suppose there is a person in the village who doesn't know by now that you're staying with me. And everyone would know that you wouldn't be wandering around by yourself this late at night. Besides, there's every reason to think that those two men would recognize you as easily as they would Angela."

Mrs. Edwards looked stubborn. "I think it's silly not to try to find out if they are in there. Couldn't we go back to Cuthberts and suggest that Per—suggest that Mr. Hetherege go there for a drink?"

"Too late," said Dame Millicent, starting the engine. "It's almost closing time now. No, let's forget it. As Angela says, there are thousands of cars like that in England."

"Millicent," said Mrs. Edwards firmly, "stop the car, please; the least we can do is to stop here and watch who comes out of the inn."

"Very well," said Dame Millicent somewhat sulkily, as she switched off the ignition. "But I think you'll find it's a waste of time."

The inadequate little light over the pub sign illuminated the front door, but it didn't reach as far as their car. "No one will see us here," said Mrs. Edwards.

In a minute they heard the church clock strike ten-thirty. No one appeared at the door. Five more minutes passed, and Dame Millicent began to fidget. At ten-forty she said sharply, "Watkins had better be more punctual about closing time, or he is going to lose his license."

As if in answer, the door of the pub opened for a little group of men, who stood in front of it talking before they bade each other goodnight and went to their separate cars. No one approached the Vauxhall.

Two more men came out together and turned toward the village in an ancient farm van. Only two cars were left now, the Vauxhall and a white Mini. Almost immediately a young man with long hair climbed into the Mini and roared off into the night.

The pub door opened again, and a man came out, but he had turned toward the lavatories before he reached the light of the sign, and his face remained invisible to the women waiting in the car. "It could be Bert," Angela said slowly. "At least, I know it isn't the tall man."

"Perhaps he is still in the inn," said Mrs. Edwards. They sat quietly, watching the pub. The door opened again, and two men stood talking, silhouetted against the lights inside, their faces indistinguishable. The sound of the door to the lavatories drew their attention. "Good night," they called.

"Good night," Mr. Applethwaite answered cheerily as he passed them and walked under the light of the sign. He unlocked the door of the Vauxhall, started the engine, and in a minute was gone back toward the village, his headlights picking out the hedges on either side of the narrow road.

"There," said Angela. "I couldn't have been more wrong. I feel like a fool for having alarmed you both. Let's go home now."

"Good night," they heard Watkins call. The man who had been talking to him answered, then stepped into the light just before it was switched off from inside the building. It was Peregrine.

He came along the road toward the car, swinging his stick. When he was even with them, he stepped up to the car and opened the door. "I say, Millie, this is most kind of you, but you needn't have waited for me. I could have walked."

"I think," said his sister with some asperity, "that you might at least ask why we're here."

"Don't be silly," he said as he climbed in. "It isn't as if this were some beastly foreign country." He managed a place for himself between Angela and Iseult. "It's our road. Now, let's go home."

CHAPTER FIFTEEN

BY THE TIME Mike got off the bus, Stevenson's car had disappeared. It had been headed in the direction of the Hall when he last saw it, but Stevenson might easily have turned off elsewhere, or even have driven straight past the Hall. There was no proof that it had been his destination.

He knew that he should telephone to Dame Millicent to let her know that he would miss dinner at Cuthberts, but it would be hard to do so without worrying her. At this late hour anything less than the truth would be unconvincing, so that she would realize it if he were lying. But to tell her the truth about what he was going to do would make her and Peregrine and Mrs. Edwards—yes, and Angela—worry unduly until he got back.

If he didn't telephone now, she would think he was rude, but when he returned later in the evening and explained what he had been up to, she would surely forgive him for a small thing like missing dinner. After all, Jim was his brother. On the whole, it was probably best not to phone.

He wished that he had stayed on the bus until after it had passed the gates of the Hall, so that he could have had a good look through them without danger of being recognized. Even a car would have been useful, but now he would have to take a chance on walking past the gates.

As he approached the park walls of the Hall, he looked down the road ahead. There was a footpath on the side opposite the Hall, and for a good part of its length it was shaded by trees that would partially hide him from passing drivers. But the path could be seen clearly from the upper windows of the dower house and of the former agent's house. If he walked close to the high wall, he would be invisible from inside the park except in passing the gates to the Hall and to the other two houses, but there were no trees or shrubberies along the entire bare length of the wall, and he could easily be seen from the road.

He shrugged, pulled up the collar of his raincoat around his ears, and started down the pathway opposite the Hall. The gates to the dower house were some thirty yards from the beginning of the wall, and he automatically looked through them as he passed, expecting to see nothing. After all, Plymson was dead, no successor had been appointed so far as he knew, and there was no reason for anyone to be in the house unless the police were still there. But the drive curved away from the gates, so that he could not see the house. If there was a car parked near it, it was certainly invisible to him.

Across the road from the main gates he stopped under the shelter of a large chestnut. The drive led straight to the front of the house, and even at this distance he could easily see that the gravel in front of the curving steps was empty. The big gates stood ajar, but there was no one about. The curtains were drawn on the front windows of the lodge, although it would not be dark for another three hours. Probably the gate keeper and his family were having their tea.

The open gates must indicate that the guard dogs were not

yet turned loose. Presumably they were normally released before dark, for Plymson had been killed while watering his
garden, and it would have made no sense for him to wait for
darkness before going to take care of the fateful begonias. Or
gloxinias, as Watkins had said. All of which seemed to indicate
that the dogs would be roaming the park when darkness fell in
another two or three hours. But how long before that they would
be turned loose was difficult to guess.

He left the shelter of the chestnut and continued toward
the far end of the wall. Originally it must have been inviting
rather than inhospitable, for it was a beautifully regular dry wall
made of warm local stone, but to its top had been added three
jagged rows of barbed wire held in place by steel posts that
leaned outward to forbid entry to the park.

As Mike had seen from the hill above Market Doddington
that morning, the park was severely, almost ruthlessly, symmetri-
cal where it bordered the road, so he was not surprised that the
drive to the former agent's house was a perfect mirror image of
the drive of the dower house. Through the gates he could see
nothing but the curve of a beech hedge bordering its drive.

He slackened his pace. He had seen nothing of interest by
coming past the Hall and park, and certainly he had not seen the
long black car that Stevenson had been driving half an hour before. Probably little would be gained by walking further. He
thought with regret of the bus that he had left so hurriedly.
From its upper deck he could have seen over the park walls.

Then he remembered the hill road from which he and Dame
Millicent had stopped to look at Market Doddington that morning. It was a perfect vantage point, not more than twenty minutes' climb from where he stood. Without further debating the
matter, he walked to the end of the front wall of the park, then
turned left and walked beneath the shelter of the side walls. A
hundred yards ahead he could see the beginning of the curve
as the narrow road led back up the hill to where he and Dame
Millicent had been earlier in the day.

At the top the view was obscured by a light haze hanging
over the valley in which the village stood. Even so, he had no
trouble in seeing the Hall and the buildings that shared the

park with it, and he was able to make out three cars parked behind the Hall, none of which was the one in which he had seen Stevenson. From where he stood he could see the entire sweep of empty driveway in front of Plymson's house; the drive of the companion house was cut from his view by the roof of the house itself. If Stevenson had parked there, his car would be completely hidden from Mike's sight. Damn! A long uphill walk, and he knew no more than he had known when he stood across the road from the gates of the Hall.

Not that he knew, even now, what he was expecting to find. Stevenson's car, perhaps. And that would probably mean that the heart of the whole intrigue surrounding Jim was still in the Hall itself. There was little doubt that Stevenson had been following him, Mike, across the ocean, in France, now in Warwickshire.

Stevenson, yes, but Jim as well? Mike hardly dared ask himself whether he expected to find Jim, although the conversation with the salesman about the recording tape made it seem at least possible. When he had first heard the tape, Mike had wondered vaguely about the time involved in recording the tape in Moscow, sending it to England, and getting it to Angela. Even with airplanes and diplomatic pouches, it had seemed as if pretty close timing had been involved. The whole arrangement would have been difficult, although probably not impossible, and he had never really doubted that it had taken place, since he had questioned neither the Russian statement that Jim was applying for asylum nor the story that he had been seen in the streets of Moscow. But, if neither story were true, there was no reason to believe that Jim had ever left England.

The more he thought about the package of recording tape, the more convinced Mike was that the reports of Jim in Moscow had to be lies. At least the official Russian statement had to be a lie, and the story of the tourists about having seen him at best a mistake. "Four or five days" the man in the shop said had elapsed since the sale of the tape. Obviously his memory wasn't to be relied upon completely; it could easily have been a week. And there was no proof that the purchase hadn't been made by a completely innocent person who happened to own an out-of-date machine like Angela's. The stubborn fact remained, however, that the only sale of that size of tape for a year or two had taken place at precisely the right time to have been used in the recording given to Angela in Paddington station.

Mike counted on his fingers. He had been in England almost two weeks now, and all but one day of that time he had been in Lower Doddington, but it was difficult to guess how long the enemy had known that he was there. He didn't see any way that they could have followed him from the east coast to Stratford, but probably there really wasn't any need for them to follow him in person; they knew he would come to the neighborhood of Market Doddington, and all that they had to do was wait for him.

For five days he had been ill at Cuthberts, without ever going out of the house, which probably meant that his trail hadn't been picked up until a week ago. He hadn't even met Angela until six days ago, and it was only five days since they had gone together to Stratford. In other words, there had been no reason until five days ago to send a threat to him through Angela. Before that they simply hadn't known each other well enough for it to make sense.

Five days. No, even less than that. They had gone to Stratford on Saturday, but it had been in the evening, and by then the camera shop would have been closed. Suppose they had bought the tape on Monday morning, and yesterday, Wednesday, the tall man had given it to her. Two days. There simply hadn't been time after buying the tape to fly it to Russia, make the recording, and return it to London. But there was plenty of time to get the tape in Stratford, make the recording in England, and give it to Angela. Plenty of time. And that must mean that Jim was in England.

He was disturbed in his calculations by a movement in the park below his observation point. A car was driving away from the former agent's house, which Dame Millicent had said was made into flats. Presumably the car had been hidden behind the house itself. The ground fog made it difficult to be sure about the appearance of the car, but it was certainly large, and it was apparently very dark in color. But Mike could not identify it until it came to a fog-free patch in the driveway. There could be little doubt: it was Stevenson's car, or at least it was almost identical with the one he had been driving. As Mike watched, it turned onto the main road toward Market Doddington, then vanished into the village.

That settled it. He had no way of following Stevenson, but at the least he would find out what he could at the Centre itself. Perhaps Jim was still hidden there, but that seemed unlikely, since it would be too dangerous for his captors to keep him there. Still, Mike had to know. He started back toward the Hall.

When he had been walking beside the park on the road leading up the hill, he had been under the unfriendly wire barrier that leaned out from the top of the wall. Not much chance of getting through that without a way of lifting himself to its level. The cutters he had bought in Stratford would take care of the wire unless it was electrified; he had noticed that the wire was not continued across the tops of the gates of the three driveways breaking the park walls, which must mean that there was no current through it. Even so, he couldn't get up to the level of the wire. The wall was eight or nine feet high, and he couldn't remember so much as a tree leaning over it, as he had assumed there always was in a proper English park.

When he reached the side wall of the park again, he stood looking down its length. Nothing to help him over it, nothing even to get him to the level of the wire, so that he could use the cutters. But he had to get over.

There had been no traffic on the side road since he had started up the hill, and he walked without undue care along the wall until he judged that he must be opposite the back gardens of the agent's house. The wall was too high for him to see even the roofs, but he felt moderately confident that he had not misjudged the distance.

The only way he could get over the wall was to take advantage of the steel barrier itself. At ten-foot intervals heavy posts had been cemented into the top of the wall, leaning out at a forty-five-degree angle to support the three heavy strands of wire. One of the posts ought to hold him.

He jammed the wirecutters and flashlight into the side pockets of his trousers, then took off his raincoat and jacket, tied them into a ball with the sleeves of the raincoat, and carried the ball across the road, where he wedged it into the rough hedge enclosing a field. He could retrieve it when he came back out of the park. His new sweater would keep him warm, and he would be free of the tails of his coat and jacket as he climbed.

At the wall once more, he stood puffing out his cheeks slightly as he wondered whether he had the agility to do what he contemplated. He had to have: there wasn't a choice. The base of the steel post was not far above his outstretched fingers when he stood on tiptoe, and he could probably grasp it if he had a run, but the lowest wire ran only two or three inches above the base, and he would lacerate his hand if he were to try to support himself there.

He took off the belt he had bought just before leaving the States, then refastened the buckle securely. He backed into the middle of the road and ran toward the wall, jumping as high as he could when he was beneath the steel post. With both hands he swung the belt and tried to slip it over the top of the post, but it hit the steel and glanced off.

Now he was puffing in earnest. He knew that his jump had been truncated by his unconscious fear of plunging into the wall as he came down. If he were to run parallel to the wall, he would have no such worry, but the angle for slipping the the belt over the post would be more difficult. All the same, it was worth a try.

This time the belt caught on the post, and he hung from it briefly to test it before he dropped to the ground. Then he jumped again for the belt with both hands and threw out his feet to the wall, bracing his rubber heels to keep them from slipping. Slowly he inched his way up into the belt until he could slip his left arm through the loop and then painfully support his weight on his armpit.

He was glad that he had had the sense to get heavy-duty wirecutters. Cringing to avoid the cruel, flapping ends of the wire, he cut through it and watched it fall away on either side of the post. He took a deep breath of relief. At least there had been no current in it. He heaved his right foot up over the post, pulled himself slowly up to the top of the wall, and quickly bent down to avoid making too much silhouette. His guess about the location of that part of the wall had been right. On the other side a line of outbuildings divided the garden from the back of the agent's house. He dropped down from the wall as lightly as he could.

As Plymson had told Mrs. Edwards, the gardens were kept in reduced order since the Hall had been taken over by the Centre, but the shrubbery was intact. A few feet from where he landed was a large clump of gorse bushes, put there in Victorian times. Keeping low, he scuttled toward them and sat beneath their shelter as he took stock of his situation.

Over the outbuildings he could see the upper floors of the house. In one of the windows a light was burning, although it would not be dark for some time. It was just after eight now, and it would probably be light until at least ten-thirty or eleven. It was always hard to realize how much later darkness fell in England in the early summer than in Connecticut.

In the distance he heard the single yelp of a dog, followed by a whole chorus of barking. It wouldn't be safe to go around the house until eleven, and by then the dogs would be loose in the park. If his earlier calculations were correct, they might be released at any moment. The thought of what had happened to Plymson made him feel cold.

But surely the dogs wouldn't be free to come into the garden surrounding this house. It had been only a freak accident that the gates to Plymson's garden were open when he was killed. Or, at least, it was certain that they were not normally kept open, even if his death had not really been an accident. Since there were flats in the old agent's house, their inhabitants would have to be free to come and go without worrying about the Dobermans, and that surely meant that the gate between the garden and the park would be kept closed at night. So long as he didn't have to go into the main part of the park, he ought to be safe from the vicious brutes.

Dogs or no dogs, he was not going to sit on the soaking

ground under dank gorse until darkness fell. From the house he was probably invisible, but if any of its occupants came into the garden, he would be trapped and almost certainly seen through the thin undergrowth.

Above all, there was no time to waste. If he were going to be spotted by someone coming into the garden, he might as well be caught reconnoitering as soaking up the morning's rain in the seat of his trousers. Now that he was within the precincts of the Centre, his first task was to find out whether Jim was prisoner there and, if possible, release him. Once he had done what he could in that direction, he could think about identifying whoever was responsible.

Keeping close to the shrubbery lining the wall, he started toward the buildings that stood between him and the house. Stumps, not yet rotted away, indicated why there had been no trees hanging over the wall. They had all been cut down, presumably to make entry difficult for trespassers like himself. Or perhaps merely to avoid maintenance.

Once he had reached the low outbuildings, he left the shrubbery and took refuge behind them, where he could not be seen from the house. They formed a continuous line of pink brick only one story high, although the roofs went up at a sharp angle, indicating that they were considerably higher inside. A line of windows at eye level pierced the brick.

When he reached the end window, he looked cautiously into it. Through wide-open modern doors on the other side of the building that had been installed to make the old stables into a garage, he could see into the courtyard behind the house. It was a deep building, and once it had clearly contained rows of horse stalls on both sides of an aisle, but the row on the other side had been removed to make room for the garage doors. Those stalls on the side on which he was standing had been left intact, since there was adequate room for a car without removing a second row. They were long stalls, built luxuriously wide for the heavy horses of the eighteenth century, their sides smooth from centuries of horseflesh rubbing against them.

Two sets of doors had been inset into the far wall on either side of the high center door that had been the original entrance to the stables. That made five roomy spaces for cars, but there was only one parked there now, and it was unfamiliar.

The steep-pitched roof sloped upward, giving the old stables a cavernous, almost cathedral-like, appearance. But it was not architecture in which he was interested now. What was more important was that there was no hiding place there, no unused room in which Jim could be kept captive. It was unlikely that anyone would try to hide Jim in one of the wooden laboratory buildings at the back of the Hall, or in the Hall itself. They were both filled daily by dozens of technicians, and unless the entire Centre was in conspiracy, it would not be safe to hide Jim there. Perhaps there were unused attics in the Hall itself, but even that seemed an unnecessarily risky place to keep a man captive.

If Jim were actually at the Centre, he must surely be somewhere in the house on the other side of the garages. Perhaps in one of the flats, although whose flat he couldn't imagine. It was difficult trying to guess when he hadn't even met anyone who worked for the Centre except Plymson and his pink-cheeked assistant. Plymson was dead, and he couldn't so much as remember the assistant's name.

The truth was that after all the trouble—perhaps even danger—of getting into the Centre, it seemed increasingly improbable that Jim could be there. Not many hiding places were available, in spite of the size of the Hall and the park. There must be a dozen places within a few miles where it would be far easier to conceal a man. A rented cottage, or the barn of some compliant farmer willing to ask no questions in return for a few hundred pounds; even the windowless buildings of the deserted American air base would serve. It was only too easy to think of innumerable places that would answer the purpose far better that any building within the park of Doddington Hall.

Nonetheless, that was where he was now, and it would be foolish not to find out what he could before he left. He took another look into the garage. Impossible to hide a man there. He turned away from the window, and as he did, he had an odd feeling of discrepancy between the length of the exterior of the building and what he had seen of its interior. Another look through the window convinced him; the last of the windows at the far end of the building must belong to a smaller room separate from the stables. Probably a tackroom in the more expansive days of the Doddingtons.

Since he had come out from under the cover of the gorse, he had not heard any cars in the driveway, and there had been no noise of doors opening or closing in the house itself. The probability that anyone would come to walk in the wet garden was pretty remote, he had to admit, in spite of his earlier fears. With no attempt at concealment except keeping near the wall of the stables, he walked to the other end of the building and looked into the last window.

The glass was dirty, and at first he could see nothing inside. As he had guessed, it was not part of the old stable, for the interior was dark except for a slight illumination from the little window through which he peered. The window itself was hinged from the top and stood open an inch or two at the bottom. Cautiously, hoping that it would not squeak, he slid his fingers behind it and levered outward. The window gave only one protesting groan, then opened out until it was horizontal.

With his head inside the building, he could see by his flashlight that it had been made into a garden shed, although the hooks and gear of an old-fashioned tackroom were still in place on the walls. It was a long, narrow room, the size of two of the stalls in the stables. Around its edges stood bags of fertilizer and garden tools. Near the far end was a large power mower. And there was no place where Jim could be hidden.

At least there was no place to hide him if he were alive. For the first time Mike seriously considered the possibility that his brother could have been murdered. At first he had believed that Jim was living in Moscow, and then the recording had proved that he was alive within the past week. However, once he had been tortured into giving up his knowledge of the research at Coronado, his usefulness to the Russians might be slighter than the embarrassment of having to deal with him.

He was a fine chemist, of course, but perhaps his potentiality was no greater than that of many young Russians. If that were so, Mike realized that there might be no reason for his captors to keep Jim alive.

He put his head inside the window once more, and though it made no sense, he called softly, "Jim!" No answer, and he hadn't really expected one, but he had somehow to keep believing that Jim was still alive. "Jim!" For a moment he felt so discouraged that he considered simply climbing back over the wall, somehow getting out of England, and then staying forever in Connecticut. But that wasn't good enough. Nothing had changed in the past few minutes except that he had suddenly considered a new possibility, so discouraging that he had almost lost his grip. Even if he were ultimately to discover that Jim was no longer alive, he owed it to his brother to make every possible effort until he knew for certain that there was no hope. Anything less would be a betrayal of Jim.

The old tackroom was empty, but that didn't make it valueless to him. He could wait there until dark before trying to investigate the house.

He hauled himself up to the window, turned his shoulders sideways, and finally hung over the sill, head down inside the tackroom. Another moment and he had inched his hips forward through the window, then he fell heavily onto a bag of fertilizer. At least, he thought, it had probably kept him from a sprained wrist or a broken arm, no matter how it smelled.

He sat down on the bag until his breath had returned, then got up to investigate the room that he had been surveying as he tried to regain his wind. Beyond the power mower were double doors of heavy oak. He pushed against them, gently at first, then harder, but they refused to open. They must be locked from the outside. For what small comfort it was, that probably indicated that they were closed for the night, and that no one would come to bother him.

Along the side wall of the room he found another door, giving access to the stables from the tackroom, but a heavy modern bar, presumably added at the conversion of the building, kept it from being opened from the stable side. Whoever was in charge of the garden was evidently so proud of his power mower that he was afraid it would be stolen.

Noiselessly he removed that bar from its housing, then stood listening. There was no sound from the other side, and at last he eased the door open a crack to look out. The solitary car still stood in its place, and there had been no change in the stables. He closed the door and replaced the bar. When darkness fell, this would be an easier exit than the window.

Reminded that the window still stood wide open, he closed it to its original position. He wouldn't miss the evening air on this chilly night, particularly as his clothes were damp from his short stay under the gorse. He wished that it had been practical to bring his raincoat over the wall with him.

It would be a long wait until it was dark, so he might as well make himself comfortable. Another bag of fertilizer laid on its side made a seat, and he leaned back against the one on which he had landed. A pity that he didn't have a little of the bourbon that Dame Millicent had bought that morning. It was only eight-thirty, and he would be cold by eleven in his damp clothing.

In spite of himself, he could not resist looking frequently at his watch. The minutes went by slowly, A quarter of nine. His stomach reminded him that he had not eaten since lunch. Three minutes before nine. Dame Millicent was probably tucking into the bourbon in front of a blazing fire. Well, perhaps not blazing in Cuthberts, but even a single strand of glowing wire would be welcome now. Maybe darkness would come early because of the cloudy skies.

In the distance he heard a clock striking, and though he knew only too well what the time was, he counted the strokes. Nine o'clock.

As if to annihilate the silence after the striking clock, another noise came through the window, the yelp of dogs. Somehow, they sounded different now, not as if they were churning around in their pens. Probably they had been released into the park. Then there was utter quiet again, and he pictured their sleek black bodies racing silently around the park in search of prey. He had always thought of himself as a dog lover, but the one dog he feared was the Doberman pinscher. To him the breed was like the drooling monsters of childish nightmare. He knew that even to save Jim he could not bring himself to venture into the park when they were running loose.

There remained the problem of how to search for Jim in the house. As he had noticed from the hill, it was not so big as the dower house, although their façades were identical. The rooms in Queen Anne houses tended to be large, and there were presumably three, at most four, in each of the three stories, which made it likely that there was one flat on each level. If Jim were there, he was probably in either the cellar or the attics. It might not be too difficult to get into the cellar, but the attics were another matter.

He shivered. The weight of his new sweater was welcome, but its thickness meant that it held dampness longer. A quarter past nine. The faint light on the floor thrown from the window behind him seemed dimmer, but perhaps that was only wishful thinking. Suddenly it darkened still more, as if a shadow had passed over the floor. He jerked his head around, but there was nothing to be seen in the window. The long wait in the dusky shed must be distorting his vision.

The faint shadow swept across the floor again. He knew this time that he was not imagining it, but the dirty panes were vacant when he turned. Slowly he stood up and watched the window as he moved into the deeper shadow near the door leading to the stables. He would like to think that the movement had been produced by the branch of a tree waving across the window, but he knew that there were no trees nearby.

As he watched, the window suddenly framed a dark face that disappeared almost before he could take in the curled ears, the glistening white teeth, and the strong jaws parted in a silent snarl. He swallowed with difficulty, his throat slowly constricting so that only a thin column of air could pass through it. The evil face materialized again, this time in half profile, the dull evening light reflected in the baleful eyes, turning them flat and golden like the eyes of a pheasant caught in the headlights of a car. And now the snarl came faintly to his ears, no louder than the sound of his own swallowing.

There was a terrible scrabbling bang on the great oak doors at the other end of the tackroom, but they held firm against the weight of the dogs hurling themselves at it. Convulsively he turned to be sure that the bar was in place locking the door into the stables, then went back to the main doors. They opened outward, and no amount of barricading would strengthen them. Momentarily he was able to think calmly enough to realize that the more the dogs thumped upon them, the less chance there was that the doors would open.

The single terrifying face flashed past the window again. The brute was leaping tirelessly on hind legs like steel springs. Up, down. Up, down. Up, down. Sooner or later he might hurl himself through the window. A leap of five or six feet was nothing to a Doberman, and probably a pane of dirty glass was no obstacle, either. Mike looked upward, but the beams supporting the roof had been covered with a wooden ceiling. There was no place to which he could climb above the level of the great leaps of the dogs. Nowhere to hide, and if he were to go out of the door into the stables, they would be upon him as they streamed through the open garage doors.

Except for the faint snarling and the loud thumps on the big doors, there was remarkably little noise. Hardly enough to attract the attention of anyone to rescue him. Or would he be rescued? If he were noticed, the dogs might be turned loose on him, and in the morning he would be found, his mauled body hardly distinguishable from Plymson's.

Without warning the thumping on the doors stopped. In the ominous silence that followed all that remained constant was the repetitive face of the Doberman in the window. Then that stopped. Nothing. The silence was worse than the sound of claws on the oak.

A key turned in the big lock of the main doors, and one of them swung open a foot or so. Mike grabbed a spade standing next to the wall. At least he would have the satisfaction of smashing the head of one of the dogs before the others fell upon him. But no dogs came through the door.

"Come out, Mr. Templeman." He stood immobile. "Come out." The voice seemed vaguely familiar. "We've called off the dogs, but if you don't come out at once, we'll let them in there."

Stiffly Mike moved toward the door and pushed it open far enough to walk through. Dim though the evening light was, it nearly blinded him after the darkness of the tackroom. The first thing that he recognized was a semicircle of dogs facing him, three sitting on each side. Their jaws were open as they panted, their eyes fixed intently on him, their haunches quivering slightly as if ready to spring at the first word of release.

Behind the three dogs on the left stood Bert. Controlling the other trio was the tall man. And between them stood Plymson's assistant, his blue eyes now hostile in strange contrast to his baby-faced complexion. Applethwaite, that was his name. Unpleasant as his expression was, Mike preferred it to the slight amusement that lay behind the eyes of the other two men.

"Take off your pullover," Applethwaite said without inflection. Mike started to speak, then stopped as his eyes fell on the glittering eyes of the dogs. Awkwardly he pulled off his sweater and put it over his arm.

"Roll up your right sleeve." He had trouble unfastening the button at the cuff. "Hurry up!" Applethwaite's voice crackled, and Mike finished rolling it up in big uneven folds.

With a gesture that looked as if he were feeling for a cigarette, Applethwaite reached into an inner pocket of his coat and pulled out a plastic container. Without hurry he opened it. He stepped forward, rubbed his left thumb over the fleshy part of Mike's arm, and plunged in the needle.

CHAPTER SIXTEEN

M IKE."

"Aw, Mom, do I have to take him with me?"

"If you don't, you can't go to the movies. You know that." Her face was stern.

"He's too little. He always cries at the sad parts."

"Don't be silly, Michael. He'll behave himself. He's your brother, and you have to take care of him."

"Do I have to?"

"Of course; I'll give you money for popcorn for both of you."

He scowled at his brother. "Wouldn't you rather stay home? You can play with my football."

"Mike."

Enraged, he kicked at a chair. His leg hurt.

His leg hurt. Not badly, but there was a dull ache. And he felt pleasantly drowsy. Otherwise all right. Then he remembered Applethwaite and the needle. He felt his right arm. A little sore, but that was all. Vaguely, without urgency, he wondered how long he had been unconscious. He stirred, his eyes fluttered open, then shut quickly. He opened them again in panic, his sleepiness evaporated. Had they blinded him? For a moment he lay rigid in unreasoning terror, before he lifted his left arm and saw the reassuring luminous dial of his watch. Eleven o'clock. But there was no way of knowing what day it was. For all he knew, he might have slept twenty-four hours.

It was the blackest night imaginable. Not so much as a stray chink of light broke the darkness. He put down his left hand again, and it touched something stiff and crinkly, as if he were lying on hay or straw.

"Mike."

The voice was soft and dreamlike, but he knew he was not dreaming. Not now.

"Jim!" he said unbelievingly, starting up onto his elbows. "Jim. Where are you, Jim?"

"Here, Mike." Jim's voice still sounded like something from dream world. "In the next stall."

Mike sprang forward, then fell as if tackled around the shoe tops, and heard a chain rattle at his ankle. He put down his hands to examine the fastening. What felt like handcuffs, attached to a chain, encompassed his ankle. "Careful," Jim said in the same unemphatic voice as Mike explored the length of chain until he found its end in a great steel ring embedded in a bar of wood.

"Where the hell are we?" he demanded furiously, then felt ashamed of his own selfishness. "Are you all right, Jim?"

"I think so," said Jim without conviction. "It's a barn or a stable. That's all I know." He sounded much closer now. "Can you stand up?"

Careful to stay within the length of chain, Mike rose to his feet and turned in the direction of Jim's voice. He stepped cautiously forward, holding his hands in front of him, until they felt smooth wood under them.

"You can reach over it if you go a little farther from the wall. Past the piece that keeps the horses' heads apart."

Slowly he passed his hands over the wood, and then they touched Jim's face. He felt the untidy hair and the thick stubble on his cheeks. "My God, I'm glad to see you."

"Sorry I got you into this," Jim's voice sounded stronger now but almost as if he were keeping tears in check. "But it's a long time since I've seen a friendly face." He laughed unsteadily. "Not that I can see much of you now."

"How long have you been here?"

"Not long. An hour or two. It's hard to guess the time in the dark. They brought me here just before they hauled you in."

Well, that answered one question. It was still the same night. "Where have you been?"

"In a house somewhere. Not very far, I think, because it took only half an hour or so to drive here. But they wouldn't let me see, of course."

"Sure you're all right?"

"I'm okay, I think, but I've been in the dark so long that sometimes I've wondered whether I could still see. How long has it been, Mike?"

An immense wave of tenderness for his younger brother swept over Mike. All the spunky, awkward enthusiasm that had made him loved by everyone who knew him was gone. He put his hand on Jim's shoulder. "Nearly three weeks."

"I've had a lot of drugs, and I've slept a lot, and it's been hard to keep track of time. I thought maybe it was several months, but my beard didn't seem long enough for that. Is—is Angela all right?"

"Fine. She'll be even better once we get you out of here." He hoped he sounded more optimistic than he felt.

"Don't count too much on that." The worst of it was that Jim didn't even seem dejected; everything came out in that damned flat tone. "I suppose she got that recording I made?"

"Yes, she did, and that's how I found you. I got your tipoff."

"Not much, was it? It was all I could think of to let you know I didn't mean what I was saying." He drew in his breath. "Does she know?"

"Sure, she does. And she's waiting for you to come back." He remembered her attack on him for seeming to be angry at Jim. "I think she'd go on waiting forever, if need be. Thank God, she won't have to." He ran his hand up and down the wooden partition. "I think I know where we are. This must be the stable behind Plymson's house."

"Could be." Jim didn't sound interested. "Did they get him?"

Mike wished he could merely have nodded his head without speaking. "Yes. Two or three days ago. Do you know what happened?"

"I suppose he found out what Applethwaite was up to, and probably he followed him to the house where they were keeping me. I heard them quarreling, and that's the last I knew about it. Did they kill him?"

"Yes." His own fate wasn't looking too promising at the moment. Evidently Applethwaite didn't waste much time.

As if he knew what Mike was thinking, Jim said, "Don't worry about yourself. They wouldn't have bothered bringing you here if they were—well, if they were going to do that to you."

"Forget it." Probably Jim didn't believe a word he was saying. It was like him, even in his present state, to try to cheer up his brother. "I'll be all right. What I want to know is how the whole thing happened. Tell me from the beginning."

There was a long pause before Jim answered. "It's hard to remember it all. It's those damned drugs they've been giving me."

"When did you first find out about Applethwaite?" Mike asked gently. If he could help Jim along, perhaps he could remember.

"I came back to my office one night fairly late to finish up some odds and ends. I had walked over after I had been reading in my room. When I went into my office, I found him with my safe open, reading what I had written up of the project I had been working on. I had even thought it might be Plymson who had been at it, but I should have known it couldn't be. After all, he would have seen it soon enough in any case. Applethwaite had always seemed such a little white mouse that it had never occurred to me to suspect him."

"What did you do when he came in?"

"He pulled a gun on me and made me go to his office with him. There he made me get down on my hands and knees on the floor and jabbed me in the ass with a needle."

"How did he get you out of the gates? The gatekeeper must have known that you came in, and he would have had a record that you hadn't gone out. Or is he working with Applethwaite?"

Once more Jim paused before answering. "I've tried to figure that one out myself. I was pretty foggy by the time he had walked me to the car. I suppose he got me into the other front seat and propped me up. That's the only way I can think of that he could have done it. The gatekeeper isn't very careful about the people he knows when they are going out. He probably saw both of us and thought nothing of it when Applethwaite turned in our passes. Anyway, I can't remember much after I got into the car. Sorry, Mike, I'm not thinking very clearly tonight."

Before Mike could answer, he was blinded by a flash of light. He covered his eyes with his hands. There was the noise of a key in a lock, then he heard Applethwaite's voice. "Have you had a pleasant family reunion?"

Mike removed his hands. After the complete darkness, the

electric light made his eyes feel as if they were being swabbed with acid. As they slowly adjusted, he could see Applethwaite, gun in hand, standing in the passageway between two rows of horse stalls. The stables were identical with those behind the agent's house, except for the boards fitted into the windows to keep sound and light from escaping, the absence of modern garage doors, and the second row of stalls. In the one next to his own stood Jim, gaunt, hairy, his lackluster eyes blinking in the light.

Abstractedly, Jim swung his gaze toward Applethwaite. "Go to hell," he said flatly, his voice mechanical and undefiant, as if long habit had taken the place of thought and feeling. "Go to hell."

"Your conversation is getting monotonous," Applethwaite answered pleasantly. "I had hoped the stimulation of being with your brother would stir you to greater verbal felicity, Dr. Templeman."

Applethwaite, Mike realized, no longer needed chain, drugs, or gun to deal with Jim. The weeks of confinement had sapped all his vitality, leaving nothing but a hopeless, passionless resistance, and he and Applethwaite had settled into the roles of the helpless and the tormentor. If Jim were ever to stir from his lethargy, it would happen only if he, Mike, could snap him out of it. His own spirits had seldom been lower, but he could betray that fact to neither Applethwaite nor Jim. "What's the matter, Applethwaite? Are you afraid of what we may have said to each other? I don't suppose you were counting on my finding you. Or, for that matter," he lied, "on who we've got lined up behind us."

"A gallant attempt, Mr. Templeman, but you don't believe that any more than I do. I think we're both sufficiently aware that you haven't gone to the authorities. They've bungled a few other things, but at least they did manage to forbid you legal entrance to the country. That's been a considerable help. In return for which, I should add, we'll save them the trouble of having to look for you when you are gone again, since you will never have been here officially."

"I didn't say anything about the authorities." Mike smiled

in what he hoped was a condescending fashion.

"Are you referring to a couple of old women? I doubt that even you take them seriously." He turned to Jim. "What did your brother say to your suggestion? Or didn't you make it?"

"Go to hell," Jim repeated, turning his head away.

"Then I'll have to state the proposition that Dr. Templeman didn't feel he could make to you. We are taking him with us to Russia, and I'd like to have you come along. Of your own volition, I mean."

"Why do you want me? I'm not a scientist."

"I had hoped that your brother would suggest that he wanted your companionship. But since he hasn't done so, apparently, I may as well say why it would be convenient for us. If you were both to be there, and if you were trustworthy enough to be allowed to be seen by visiting Americans or Englishmen, it would remove a certain amount of international friction by suggesting that your joint removal to Russia had been part of a plan in which you both participated."

"Sorry," said Mike, "I don't like traveling. Least of all with traitors. And certainly not when it's only a front for a pipsqueak like you."

"Steady, Mr. Templeman. I've got a certain admiration for your urbanity, and I'd hate to lose it. Don't begin talking like your brother. Naturally, we'd be glad to give you something in return. Your brother has been uncooperative with us so far. We offered him his freedom in return for putting together the results of the research of his team, but he has refused, so we've got no choice except to take him with us. Eventually, I can promise you, he'll come around to our way of thinking. However, we'd like those results as soon as possible, before the experiments can be repeated by his team. We think that your presence and your urging might make him come around sooner than he might otherwise do. And—how shall I say it?—with less damage to him. In return for your joint cooperation we would give him his own experimental laboratory, freedom to do the kind of work he would like, and a more than comfortable income and style of living."

Mike reflected. "And it would also act as a deterrent to

scientific information shared by the U. S. and Great Britain, wouldn't it? That's what you're after, isn't it? That's as important as the research itself."

A brief smile crossed Applethwaite's face. "You're intelligent as well as urbane, Mr. Templeman. I don't deny that the thought had crossed the minds of some of our people."

The stable door creaked, and Applethwaite turned his head briefly. "Come in," he shouted. Bert and the tall man entered quietly, closed the door behind them, and lounged against one of the stalls. "We won't be long."

"You better hurry up," the tall man said laconically.

"Don't worry. We haven't got much more to say." He looked at Mike again. "What do you think?"

"What's in it for me? As I've said, I don't think I'd enjoy myself living with people like you."

"First of all, better treatment for your brother. But, in addition to that, you would be well taken care of, as well. You would have an opportunity to have any kind of job that would suit you best. Or, if you preferred not to work, you wouldn't need to. You can be sure that we have every intention of treating you well. After all, you would be our major showpieces as distinguished Americans who had come over to our side."

"Me? Distinguished? Cut the crap, Applethwaite."

Jim had been listening without betraying any expression on his face. At last he spoke. "Don't do it, Mike. For God's sake, don't do it."

Applethwaite reached into his pocket and took out the packet that held the hypodermic needles. "Better be quiet, Templeman." Jim hung his head and was silent.

Trying not to show the horror he felt at Jim's submission, Mike looked at Applethwaite again. "When would I have to go?"

"Tonight. We've already waited too long for you. We knew that if we warned you away you'd be sure to fall into our hands, but we had hoped that you would be quicker about it."

Mike yawned elaborately. "Afraid I'll have to decline. I haven't got any reservations for tonight."

Applethwaite's mouth twisted up in appreciation. Or was it

pleasure at the thought of breaking down Mike's resistance? "I think we could take care of the reservations for you."

"And," asked Mike, "what happens if I refuse to go?"

Applethwaite held up his hand against the light and studied the pattern of his fingers before he spoke. "You ask very awkward questions. However, I think I must tell you that we have already let you know too much, and that it would be necessary to kill you before we leave. I do hope you won't push us that far."

Mike shrugged and kept his voice under control as he replied. "Into each life some rain must fall, as they say. I suppose you must mean it. You killed Plymson, didn't you?"

"He did get in our way, and we took steps to prevent his interference. Not a very pretty death. But I suppose that sort of thing wouldn't bother you. You're a brave man if that's true. I know what those dogs are like; Bert here and Harry trained them."

"You dirty bastard!" It was Jim, his voice stronger now than it had been, stiffened by emotion.

Without answering, Applethwaite reached into his pocket, took out the packet again, and nodded to the two men behind him. They came forward, Bert took the packet, and they moved without speaking toward Jim. "Go to hell," he said defiantly, but his eyes were glassy with fear.

Mike watched helplessly as the two men seized Jim, who had no strength to fight back. The tall man pinned his arms behind his back and Bert plunged the needle into his leg. "Oh, God," Jim whispered. The tall man kept his hold on Jim's arms until his eyelids began to flutter.

"He's all right now," said Bert, and the tall man released his grip. Jim sank weakly into a sitting position in the straw of his stall, then slumped sideways.

"You filthy little white slug," Mike said to Applethwaite. "I don't give a damn what you do to me; I'll never cooperate with you now."

Applethwaite looked at his watch. "We haven't got much time, but I'll give you one more chance. I swear to you, Templeman, that you'll get good treatment if you come with us willingly. If you don't . . ." He shrugged.

Wearily Mike echoed Jim's recurrent words. "Go to hell."

"You've had your last chance, and you turned it down," said Applethwaite briskly. "I haven't got time to waste in argument." He started toward the door. "Get him ready. I'll get the car." The door closed behind him.

From his pocket the tall man took a bundle of nylon cord. He unfastened the lock on Jim's feet, neatly tied them together, rolled him onto his back, and fastened his hands behind him. Still without speaking, he and Bert picked up Jim's unresisting body and carried it to the door, where they dropped it without care onto the floor.

They came back and stood looking at Mike. "Your turn," said Bert. "We won't hurt you if you don't give us any trouble. What do you say?"

"All right," said Mike stonily. A single man with his leg fastened by a chain would never be a match for two.

As Bert entered the stall, all Mike's caution vanished, and he could not resist swinging a fist at him. With a surprising grace, worthy of a dancer, Bert ducked the blow and seized his arm. Instantly the tall man had grabbed Mike's other arm. He pulled it back, then forced it upward in an agonizing twist. "Okay, Bert."

Bert tied Mike's hands behind his back before bending to open the lock. The tall man kept his grip on Mike's arm and force-marched him to the door, where they stood waiting beside Jim's inert body. Bert fitted a gag into Mike's mouth and tied it into place with a handkerchief.

In a minute Mike heard a car outside the door. Its engine was switched off, the lights in the stable were turned off from the outside, and Applethwaite came in, leaving the door open. "Let's go."

From the black interior of the building Mike looked out into the night. The damp darkness had given way to an unstained sky and a nearly full moon. Bert and Applethwaite picked up Jim and carried him out. Mike watched them put him through the back door of the familiar blue Vauxhall and dispose him on the floor. "Start moving," said Applethwaite, nudging Mike's back with the muzzle of his gun. "Get into the middle of the back seat."

Bert and the tall man sat on either side of him, their feet casually on the unconscious Jim. Applethwaite got into the driver's seat. Without turning on the lights, he started the engine and drove the car carefully along the back driveway into the park. When they reached the gate, Bert hopped out and opened it, then got in again. Mike noticed that he had not closed the gate.

It was nearly a quarter of a mile from the drive gate of the dower house to the Hall, and they drove in silence about half that length before Applethwaite stopped the car. The tall man rolled down his window, and Bert took off Mike's gag. For a moment there was nothing except the tall man's high, strong whistle. He repeated it, then opened the door and stepped out into the drive. "Get out," said Bert and pushed Mike toward the door.

Briefly Mike resisted, then the tall man grabbed his legs and pulled him out, his head and shoulders bouncing cruelly. "Stand up," said Bert and hoisted him by the arms.

Applethwaite opened the driver's door and leaned out. "I hope the dogs are hungry tonight," he said.

The tall man whistled again before he turned to Mike and stood looking at him with a malicious smile. Then he drew back his fist and hit him as hard as he could in the stomach.

As Mike slumped to the ground, he felt Bert cutting his bonds. The two men sprang into the car, slammed the door, and over his desperate attempts to get his wind back, Mike heard the car turn around and race back toward the dower house. A long clear whistle floated back to him as the sound of the car receded.

CHAPTER SEVENTEEN

L<small>ATER HE REALIZED</small> that he could not have lain there more than two or three minutes at most, but at the time it seemed that hours were passing. When he opened his eyes, a red curtain hung before them, obscuring the dappled patches of shadow and moonlight, and when he closed them, pain shot rockets of searing light across the eyeballs. The muscles of his stomach felt as if they had been kicked by a stallion. Worst of all was the effort to get his breath. After each shuddering gasp, he wondered whether he could ever find the strength to breathe again, whether all his internal organs had been ruptured.

Yet he had to get up. At any moment he might see the dogs racing noiselessly toward him, their black bodies taking shape only as they displaced patches of moonlight. Or he might not see them at all, never be aware of their arrival until their glittering teeth sank into his unresisting flesh.

As if his body were not his own, he willed it upward until he was on his feet, still unable to straighten out his agonized crouch and stand erect. Hands pressed against his abdomen, he inched forward. Ahead of him stood a smallish tree, not more than twenty feet tall. If only he could get there before the dogs arrived, he might be sufficiently recovered to climb out of their way.

His head was swimming, and he had to stop, for fear that he would totally black out ten feet short of the tree. If the dogs were making any noise, he could not hear it above the sound of his own gasping. In a moment he was able to open his eyes without having the park swim in circles, and he staggered drunkenly on.

The branches of the tree grew almost down to the ground. He rested his forehead against the pale bark before he attempted to lift one foot. Irrelevantly he wondered what kind of ornamental tree it was. Magnolia? Perhaps, but there ought to be blossoms at this time of the year. Or were the seasons different in England?

His hands were trembling so hard that he could hardly clasp them around the trunk. He plunged a foot randomly on the lowest branch, two feet away from the trunk, and heard the ripping of the branch as he fell onto the ground.

Supporting himself by the trunk, he stood up again and put his other foot on the next branch, his shoe touching the trunk. Gingerly he pulled himself up until the branch was supporting his weight. Even if he managed to get a few feet up, he might pass out and crash to the ground. He held on until the leaves stopped dipping and swaying. One more step. If the dogs arrived as he was climbing, they could attack from the back, and he would be even more helpless than he had been on the ground.

Miraculously the branches held as he went on. He couldn't begin to guess how long it was taking. Turning carefully around, he sat on a branch and looked down. He was six or seven feet off the ground, but he doubted that the branch on which he sat was high enough to protect him from the jaws of a springing Doberman.

The muscles of his abdomen were burning, but his breathing was noticeably less painful. If he had to sit the rest of the night in the tree, he might be able to keep consciousness, braced into the crotch of a branch and the trunk. He went up two more branches and looked back. That should be enough. Had he brought his belt from the wall, where he had climbed into the park, he could have fastened himself to the trunk. As it was, he would have to hold on with his arms until morning. How long? Eight hours? At least. It must be midnight by now. He sagged against the trunk.

Gradually his head cleared, and his breath came more regularly. He wondered where the dogs were. The park was large, but the piercing whistle could surely have been heard by the keen ears of the Dobermans. And they should have been here by now, however distant the corner of the park in which they were when he had been knocked down.

Though the moon was out now, the ground was still damp from the rain of the day, and his scent would lie heavy in the wet grass. The dogs would have no trouble in finding him, and they could see him up the tree in the moonlight.

There was a rustling in the grass under the black shadow of a nearby oak. Then a figure emerged into the moonlight, swinging a stick, the face obscure in the shade of a shapeless hat. The man stopped, bent over, and put a wildflower into his buttonhole as he straightened up.

"Edwards!" The voice was familiar but for the moment unrecognizable.

"Templeman! Michael!"

"Peregrine. Mr. Hetherege." He was dawdling along as if he were out for a country stroll, and at any moment the dogs might throw themselves upon him.

Peregrine's face turned upward to him, washed smooth of expression by the moonlight. "Good heavens, man, what are you doing up that tree? You'll ruin it if you're not careful. It was Teddy Doddington's favorite magnolia."

"For God's sake, climb up here as fast as you can. You haven't got a second to waste." The old fool would be killed before he knew what had happened.

Peregrine was directly below him now, and he could see the look of incredulity. "No, thanks, I gave up that sort of thing when I was sixteen. If you don't mind my saying so, I think you should too. At your age."

"The guard dogs are coming. For the love of heaven, get up here out of their reach."

"Don't be ridiculous." He adjusted the flower in his buttonhole. "They're on the other side of the park, and they'll be occupied for hours. Now climb down, like a sensible chap. We haven't got all night, you know."

"Are you sure?"

"Shouldn't say it if I weren't. Come on, let's go to the car." He was beginning to sound testy, as he occasionally did when he thought his sister was making a fool of herself. He swung his stick in mild impatience.

In spite of himself Mike began descending the tree. At last he was on the ground, still unable to stand totally erect.

"What's the trouble? Kick you in the crutch, did they?"

"No, stomach."

"Belly's as bad as the balls, I always say. I remember once in Arabia—never mind, don't suppose you want to hear about that now. Can you walk?"

Mike nodded, and Peregrine casually drew his arm up over his own shoulders. "Lean on me. Think you could get over the wall? Damned high. Took me ten minutes or more. Bad shape these days. Damn old age."

"I doubt it." Doubt it, hell; he knew he couldn't climb a wall.

"Can't go through the gate. Out of the question."

"Let's go out by the dower house."

"Isn't that where they went with their car?"

Mike nodded. "But I don't think they were going to stay. They were clearing out."

"Makes sense." Without further ado Peregrine turned down the drive up which the Vauxhall had come, supporting Mike without visible effort as he walked. "We'll have to go down the road to get the car, but it's easier than going over the wall. For you, at least."

Damn the man, thought Mike. He was at least thirty years his senior, and he was as casual as if they were off for another drink at the White Hart. His own spine still prickled occasionally at the thought of the dogs. "How do you know those Dobermans aren't going to come now?"

"Sex."

"Sex?"

"Yes. Good healthy dogs. Love it. Remember those damned silly paper pants Millie put on her bitch to keep her from spoiling the furniture while she's on heat? The bitch, I mean."

Mike nodded.

"Gathered up a damned great pile of used ones and brought them with me. Whew!" He grimaced. "Can't imagine what they see in her, myself. Still, there you are. Threw them over the wall, and when I got down, they weren't even interested in me. Just fighting each other. Shouldn't be surprised if a few of them are dead in the morning. Eaten up. Way of the world, you know."

Peregrine walked in silence, Mike limping beside him, until they reached the gate. "Got any idea where they went? Don't suppose they told you, but you're an intelligent man."

"It's too late to do anything ourselves. The best idea would be to call the police, and they might be able to stop them at Heathrow airport. They're leaving for Russia tonight. The police might at least be able to get Jim off the plane." Mike turned to be sure the gate was locked. At least he could stop thinking that he sensed the silent rush of the dogs, when they finally tired of worrying at Iseult's discarded lingerie.

"Must be mistaken. Can't leave tonight."

"They said they were leaving, and I'm sure they meant it." The dower house and stables were dark, the driveway empty. By now Applethwaite and the others must be miles from Market Doddington.

"Last flight's at twenty past nine in the morning. Taken it several times myself. Miserable hour. Too late now, in any case. Well past midnight."

When they reached the main road, Peregrine turned toward the village. "Car's down this way. Funny thing you should think they were flying tonight."

As they went to the car, Mike told Peregrine about Applethwaite's offer to take him with Jim. "At least, I assumed they would be flying. Perhaps they're going by ship."

Peregrine considered. "Possible, I suppose, but I doubt it unless they were going by private boat directly to Russia. Otherwise, inconvenient for them to get your brother through the different frontiers. Might manage to put him in a box and sneak him aboard their own ship. God knows which port they might be using. Sure you want me to call the police? Awkward for you, but they might get your brother."

Mike shook his head wearily. "I don't care about me if they can find Jim. And, if they do, they probably wouldn't be too rough on me." Suddenly he straightened up, oblivious of the pain in his stomach muscles. "It wouldn't be any more difficult

for them to take off illegally in a plane than it would be to
stow Jim aboard a ship without his being seen. Why couldn't
they do that?"

"International airports are too busy. They'd be spotted, of
course."

"They don't need an international airport if they're not being
cleared by Immigration. All they need is a runway." He and
Peregrine looked at each other, then their heads nodded in
unison. "A deserted runway," he said slowly. "Big enough for
a small plane."

"Nether Otford?"

"That's what I was thinking. Come on, we'll have to hurry."
He started to run, then doubled over in pain.

"Easy, old man, Car's only a hundred yards away." Peregrine took his arm and guided him briskly over the remaining
distance. He unlocked the door of the car and slid into the
driver's seat, while Mike got into the other door.

"Isn't this Dame Millicent's car?"

Peregrine was having trouble starting the engine and did
not answer until it had sprung into life. "Silly little contrap-
tion, but I didn't want her to take it herself. She'll be damned
angry when she discovers that I took it. Hates having anyone
drive it." He patted his pocket. "And she can't use mine. Got
the keys here."

After fiddling with the gear lever, he finally let in the
clutch, and the tires squealed as they shot forward. He rapidly
picked up speed, the motor roaring louder and louder, but
still he had not shifted gears. Mike looked at the speedometer.
Forty-five. "Don't you think you ought to shift?" he asked.

"Too much trouble. Never could figure out how this thing
worked." The sound of the engine was ominous.

"Why don't you let me drive? I've driven this kind of car
before." It was an out-and-out lie, but he surely couldn't do
worse than Peregrine. "I'm afraid we might ruin it before we
got there."

"Nonsense." He steered his way around a bicycle and its
rider, whose face shone moonlike with surprise in the lights.
"You haven't got an English license."

"I've got an international license." The pain of his stomach had diminished sufficiently for Mike to laugh inwardly at worry over a license at this point in the illegal proceedings in which he was engaged.

The tires squealed again as the car stopped. Peregrine opened his door and climbed out. "In this case, I think it would be all right."

When Mike had taken over the wheel, he asked, "How did you ever find me? You didn't know where I was going."

"Two and two. Millie found out that you had got onto the bus in Stratford. And you never got back. Missed dinner. Roast lamb with mint sauce. Pity. Still, you may get some cold. So Market Doddington seemed the obvious place for you to get off the bus. Apple pie, too. Thought I'd better have a look, so I nipped out of the back door without telling Millie. Or that pretty little Mrs. Edwards. They would have wanted to come. Too dangerous. Shouldn't say it about my own sister, but Millie's damned nosy. No place for a woman. Or women. They're probably still trying to guess how you got off at the wrong bus stop." He stopped and began to whistle to himself. Presumably he considered that his telegraphic style had conveyed all the information wanted, or, at least, needed.

"But why did you come to the Centre?"

"Obvious place in Market Doddington. Besides, there was that Applethwaite."

Mike waited, but there was nothing more forthcoming. "What about him?"

"Never did like him. Poured his own drink at Millie's party and gave me the wrong name. Then he was in the White Hart tonight. Didn't tell Millie that."

"Tonight?"

"Came in about a quarter before ten and stayed until closing time. Didn't talk to anyone and didn't seem to like the beer. Had to be up to no good. Thought perhaps something had happened to you, and that he was establishing an alibi. He's the type. I was sloping around the park when I saw the car coming from the dower house, so I hid until it was gone. And that's when I found you."

Mike slowed down as he turned into the lane leading to the deserted airport. Bad weather had dug enormous holes in the surface, filled tonight with water from the day's rain. He steered carefully around them. A broken axle would be the least he could expect if a wheel slipped into one of them. The gravel and mud had merged into a stiff mixture. "Look. Aren't those fresh tire marks?"

"Looks like it. Must be Applethwaite." Peregrine began whistling to himself again. "Intelligent, isn't she?"

"Dame Millicent? Of course. She's a distinguished scholar." It wasn't like Peregrine to speak that way of his sister.

"No, no, don't be a damned fool. Not Millie. Mrs. Edwards."

"Indeed she is."

"Pretty little thing, too." Peregrine lapsed into contemplation. "Got a gun, Templeman?"

"God, no," said Mike in surprise. "Have you?"

"Don't be ridiculous. Of course I haven't got one. Against the law. But I thought all Americans carried them."

The road came to an abrupt halt, cut off by a large steel gate confronting them in the headlights. "Probably locked," said Peregrine, "but I'll have a look." He hopped briskly out of the car and bent down at the gate, the shiny seat of his tweed trousers reflecting the lights. In a moment he straightened up and began opening the gate.

"It had been padlocked," he said cheerily as he returned, "but someone had sawed through the chain."

Mike drove through the grove of small trees that bordered on the buildings and hangars at one end of the deserted air field. In the moonlight they looked ghostly, their paneless windows black against the discolored aluminum of the siding. One leg of the old control tower had collapsed, and the box on top sloped drunkenly. Nearby a ragged piece of silk attached to a stick was all that remained of a wind sack. The single runway, black under the moon, ran straight away from the buildings until it disappeared in the distance, bordered on either side by high, uncut grass.

It all looked empty, as deserted as it had been since the

last day of its occupation, when the Americans had finally moved out. Not a sign of Applethwaite anywhere. He stopped the car. They had made a bad choice, coming here, and by the time they got back to a telephone, it would probably be too late to alert the authorities.

Yet the old field provided plenty of places where the Vauxhall could be hidden: in the deep shadows beside any of the buildings, even in the vast, deserted hangars themselves.

"Listen!" Peregrine rolled down his window.

Mike could hear nothing. "What is it?"

Peregrine put a finger to his lips, and in a moment Mike heard the faint sound of engines. The noise increased until it seemed to fill the sky above them, then passed over and diminished, although it was still clearly audible.

In a minute or two the sound increased again, and then, at the far end of the long runway, there was a sudden blaze of light that came closer and closer to the ground. When the lights looked as if they were going to burrow into the pitted macadam surface, they suddenly straightened out and pointed directly up the runway at the hangars near Mike and Peregrine. Then the lights were switched off. In the moonlight Mike could see the plane rushing toward them, then reducing its momentum.

"Sweet Christ," he said in reluctant admiration. "It takes a damned good pilot and lots more guts than I've got to make a landing like that." He let in the clutch and drove the little car into the shadow of a hangar. "Let's get out."

His foot had hardly touched the ground when there was a flash from the window of the hangar, followed by the noise of a gun that was scarcely distinguishable from the bang at the front of the car. "Bother," said Peregrine furiously. "Got a tire. Millie will skin me alive."

Immediately came another gunshot, followed by a third shot that blew out the other front tire. "Get back in the car," a voice called, audible over the noise of the plane, now taxiing up the runway. "I'll shoot either one of you who tries to leave it." It was Bert's voice, Mike was sure.

"Better do what the fellow says," Peregrine muttered as he got back into the car. More slowly Mike climbed back into the driver's seat. They couldn't drive the car with two flat front tires, and they would be easy targets if they were to leave it. There was nothing more that they could do. To have come so far, and now to have to sit helplessly while Jim was flown off into the night, probably never to come back. He slumped over the wheel, and tears of combined pity and frustration forced themselves out of his eyes.

The plane came to a halt, but the engines were still turning at what sounded like full speed. In the clear moonlight he could see a door open and steps put down to the runway. But no one came down them.

Suddenly from the ruined doors of the hangar nearest them a car without lights streaked out onto the runway. The sound of the plane's engines had masked the starting of the Vauxhall. A shape appeared at one of the car's windows, followed by the sound of a gun, then the faint zinging of a bullet above their heads.

"Come on," said Mike, jumping out, "They're gone."

The car jerked to a halt, and another bullet sang past his ears. He and Peregrine threw themselves down in the long grass, and the car started again. It went directly to the plane and stopped. Mike saw three figures jump out and begin passing in luggage. He wondered if it would be safe to run toward the plane, then dismissed the idea. It was too far without a car. By the time he could get there, the plane would be gone. And Jim with it.

The three figures converged at one side of the car, then turned toward the plane, carrying what looked like a large parcel. Jim. His body was passed up the ladder, one of the men slammed the door of the car, and they all climbed into the plane. The steps were drawn in and the door fastened.

Awkwardly the plane swung around, away from the deserted car, and faced back in the direction it had come along the runway. There was a pause as the engines roared, followed by the kind of shudder that precedes a small plane's launching itself into a takeoff run.

"Sorry, Michael." Peregrine reached over and touched his arm. "We did all we could."

CHAPTER EIGHTEEN

Oh, God," said Mike and buried his head in the grass. He had been able to maintain his equanimity when he thought that Jim was already in Russia, but it was intolerable to have seen him in England and then have to watch the plane lift off of the ground and head for Moscow or whatever intermediate point where it might touch down for more fuel. "Oh, God!" He hoped that Jim was still mercifully unconscious.

"Look, Templeman, look!"

At the urgency in Peregrine's voice he lifted his head. Halfway down the length of the runway a light was shining across the macadam. As he watched, it swung around and pointed directly up the runway at the plane, still quivering in its readiness for the takeoff run. For a moment the restrained movement of the plane reminded Mike of the horrible alertness of the Dobermans as he had come out of the stable.

The light was gently bouncing up and down as it started purposively toward the airplane. It was not a strong light—certainly nothing like so bright as those on the plane had been—but it prevented Mike from seeing what it was mounted on. Whatever it was, it stayed firmly in the middle of the runway, slowly closing the hundred-yard gap between it and the plane. So long as it kept its position, there was no room for the plane to pass it on the runway, and the grass on either side was much too long for a takeoff.

Without warning the plane began to move slowly forward, its two propellers still in motion, and its lights suddenly flooded the runway. "Good Lord, it's Millie!" Mike heard

Peregrine whisper almost inaudibly.

The blanching lights of the plane illuminated her like the sun at midday. Above the mutinous waves of gray hair rode the indomitable red hat. One hand was shielding her eyes from the glare while the other guided Scrogg's tractor majestically into the path of the airplane. Through the windscreen of the tractor's cab Mike could see Iseult on the passenger's seat, turning her head in curiosity from side to side.

Peregrine was already on his feet, running in the direction of the two machines. "Jump, Millie," he yelled at the top of his voice. "Jump!" In spite of the pain it gave him, Mike raced after him. At the edge of the runway they stopped together; there was nothing they could do now. "Jump!" Peregrine called hopelessly. They both knew she could not hear him.

If she were to stall the tractor in its present position and jump out of it, the plane would be blocked, but she looked as if she had no intention of leaving the controls. The gap between the tractor and the plane was rapidly shrinking as they continued their deliberate way toward a meeting, like a pair of medieval knights advancing toward each other down the length of the lists.

"They'll cut her to ribbons." Peregrine's hand squeezed Mike's arm until it hurt. The propellers were on a level with the cab, and Mike knew how quickly they would rip through the flimsy housing of the tractor. What it might do to the propellers was another matter: perhaps they would be ruined by the impact, so that the plane could not take off. Surely the pilot must be thinking the same thing, but the gap was closing inexorably. Another minute would mean the end of Dame Millicent.

By now every detail of her face was plain in the blinding light. She turned her head slightly to the side and her mouth opened as if she were shouting, but they could not hear her above the roar of the combined engines.

Suddenly from the rear of the tractor cab a great angled arm arose, the end bearing a circle of shiny steel blades reflecting the plane lights as it revolved. From where Mike and Peregrine were standing it looked like a rival propeller.

The arm swung over the cab, and the blades projected high in front of the tractor. "It's her blessed mowing machine," said Mike incredulously.

If the plane were to run into Dame Millicent's rural man-of-war now, it would still demolish it, but the crash would certainly ruin the plane as well. Mike held his breath as the strip of black between them shrank. Not more than ten yards separated them when the plane put on its brakes.

Dropping her left hand from her eyes, Dame Millicent whirled the steering wheel sharply to the right, and the tractor swung across the runway in front of the plane, then turned to the left again and veered back to the side of the plane. Standing on the mowing machine, her hands working at the controls, was Florence Edwards.

"Florence!" Peregrine shouted. By now they were so close that she heard his voice and smiled briefly in his direction before looking down at the controls again. "Bloody sister," he said more quietly. "Did she have to bring Florence with her?"

"She's lost it," Mike said despairingly. Once Dame Millicent was at the side of the plane, the pilot could slide back a window and shoot at her, or he could ignore her and take off. Either way she had made a tactical error.

A shot rang out, but neither Dame Millicent nor Florence Edwards seemed to have been hit. "Now, Florence." Dame Millicent's voice rang out over the din. "Now, Florence. Now!" Now!"

The plane began moving forward, and Dame Millicent turned the tractor directly at it. The mowing disc came down in a great arc, and as the tail of the plane was level with the tractor, Mike heard a horrible metallic crash. The blades of the mower bit into the light metal of the tail assembly, and a great piece fell to the ground. The plane came to an abrupt halt.

"Good girl, Florence," Dame Millicent bellowed. "Have another go." She swung the tractor around for a better approach. Florence Edwards whirled the two wheels of the controls and the blades chewed off a second piece of the tail assembly. Iseult was leaping around her seat in excitement, and Dame Millicent let out a hoarse, unarticulated whoop. Peregrine jumped up and down at Mike's side, shouting equally incomprehensibly.

Dame Millicent had swung away from the plane after the second encounter. "Millicent," they heard Florence shouting, "turn her around and let me have another chance. Please, Millicent."

The engines of the plane were cut off, leaving only the noise of the tractor. Then, above its sound, Mike heard the roar of motors from behind him, and headlights swept over him as four cars raced out of the road by which he and Peregrine had come. They passed him and swiftly circled the plane and the tractor. As they slammed to a halt, the doors of the cars exploded, and the runway was full of policemen.

"It's the cavalry arriving. The marines have landed," Mike howled in exultation.

"No," said Peregrine reprovingly. "Local constabulary. We don't have cavalry any longer." Mike swung around and met a twinkling gaze. "Sorry, Templeman. Sense of humor out of place, I suppose."

Florence Edwards was wheeling in the arm of the mowing machine as Dame Millicent drove her juggernaut toward them, waving. "Florence," shouted Peregrine, "here I am."

But Mike's gaze was fixed upon the plane. The door opened, and down the ladder came Applethwaite, followed by Bert and the tall man, then, after a slight pause, a stranger. Probably the pilot, Mike thought, wondering why Jim hadn't yet appeared. The four men disappeared into a circle of uniforms, then two policemen detached themselves from the group and climbed into the plane. In a minute they reappeared in the door with Jim between them. He was blinking in the headlights of the cars, but he climbed down the steps without support. Thank God, Mike thought as he started toward him.

"Wait a minute, Mr. Templeman. Wait until the others have been searched for guns." Mike spun around to look into the face of Stevenson.

Beside him stood Angela, her eyes fixed hungrily on Jim. Then she turned and smiled at Mike. Holding out her arms, she came toward him and put one arm around his neck while the cast on the other pointed straight up. "Thanks, Mike. Thanks for everything." Drawing back, she looked up at him. "And I'm sorry."

Mike nodded. There was nothing to say.

By the plane he could see the policemen bundling Applethwaite and his accomplices into the black cars. "Is it all right to go now, Mr. Smith?" Angela asked.

Stevenson nodded. Swiftly she bent and threw off her shoes. The next instant she was running toward Jim.

"Smith?" Mike asked.

With a smile Stevenson shrugged his shoulders. "Not really. But it isn't Stevenson, either. You've been a lot of help, Mr. Templeman. And a lot of trouble, too. Tomorrow I'll go with you to the Home Office and we can straighten out your entry permit. Right now, don't you want to see your brother?"

When he turned, Mike could see Jim holding Angela in his arms. Without haste he started toward them. Better give them a minute or two by themselves.

By the tractor's side Dame Millicent was walking Iseult. On the other side Florence, eyes closed, was tentatively holding up her face while Peregrine bent to kiss her. As Peregrine himself might have said, Mike thought, there seemed to be a damned inordinate amount of kissing tonight. It didn't look as if Blandinsville would be seeing much more of Florence.

Jim was still holding Angela as he came up to them. He coughed, and Jim looked up. "Good Lord, Mike, I'm glad to see you."

Once more Mike found himself nodding for want of words. At last he managed to say, "I'll get you another bottle of bourbon. I seem to have lost the one I brought you from home."

Jim smiled abstractedly. Somehow, his heart didn't seem fastened on bourbon right now.

The police cars had moved off, with the prisoners inside, then stopped by Stevenson or Smith or whatever his name actually was. "Yes, sir," he heard one of the policemen saying.

Suddenly Mike felt as he had on that day when he was ill

in Stratford, lonely, desperately lonely. No one for him to kiss. Not even anyone to talk to, and the mission on which he had come to England was over now. Things had somehow sagged, gone flat.

"Stay, girl," he heard Dame Millicent saying. She closed the door of the tractor cab on Iseult, who had resumed her seat inside. At least he could talk to Dame Millicent. He started toward her, but she had already begun marching firmly in the direction of Smith.

"Wait," he called. He didn't want to be totally alone.

"Michael, how nice to see you," she said, as if welcoming him to a party. "I was just going to tell Mr. Smith that I'd be glad to take you back with me on the tractor. I don't think there will be room for you in his car."

"I can't tell you how much I'd like that," he said wholeheartedly.

Her brow contracted. "Have you got any idea where my car is? Peregrine took it, and I can't get a word out of him. All he wants to do is to talk to Florence."

"Not the haziest," he said in breezy imitation of Peregrine. He could tell the truth tomorrow. In the meantime it might be wise to change the subject. "How did you ever think of coming here on that wonderful tractor?"

"Peregrine," she said with a sniff, "stole my keys after we had decided where you must have gone. The unfeeling brute took my car, so that I'd have to stay at home and miss all the fun. So I naturally phoned the police and told them all I knew. Mr. Smith rang back, and he said that he thought they might be coming here to the airport; he offered to take Angela with him, but he refused to let Florence and me come. So, of course, we went by bicycle to Scroggs's farm and took the tractor. Oh, dear, I suppose I'll have to explain to him tomorrow. He'll be furious."

The policeman who was talking to Smith saluted, climbed back into his seat, and the procession of cars moved away. Hardly had they disappeared when another pair of headlights appeared in the lane. Bouncing over the ruts came an ancient Land-Rover. As it ground to an abrupt stop, Scroggs jumped out, howling with fury. "Where's my tractor?" he demanded of Dame Millicent. Mike turned away. She would have to deal with this herself.

Above Scroggs's angry accusations Mike heard a confused sound of yelping. In spite of himself he jumped. It sounded as if the Dobermans had been released at last and had followed him here.

Down the lane, in full tongue, came a dark Alsatian. Immediately behind him ran a yowling collie. In quick succession Mike was passed by two mongrels, a boxer, and a shaggy creature that he decided was either a St. Bernard or a small Shetland pony. Far to the rear panted a fat and arthritic spaniel in imminent danger of a heart attack.

Hesitating only to snap at each other, they raced to the tractor and began running around it in erratic circles. Snugly and smugly ensconced behind its doors sat Iseult, yapping encouragement to her admirers.

"Come on, Templeman," said Peregrine as he approached with Florence on his arm. "We'll have to rescue her from the heathen hordes." He paused, took aim, and brought his stick down on the boxer. The dog fell to the ground, recovered itself, and headed for the trees, yipping. "As I told you the other day," he resumed, calculating the approach of the Alsatian, "put your money on the lop-eared mongrel."